CHAPTER 1 - LUDER

I pulled into the parking bay close to the door. Stepping out, I straightened my suit jacket as I glanced up to the second floor. Let's hope this meeting goes as planned. I still couldn't believe my entire guard team was down with the same virus. It almost seemed like it could be a sign. Yet, I'd never been one to cancel a meeting or show fear.

The building shone brightly in the early morning sun, almost blinding me. It was one of the more modern buildings in Miami, and the top part was made entirely of glass. The bottom floor, however, appeared to be a bit older. I wondered how long after the first floor, the second floor was added.

This had nothing to do with my meeting, but development had always intrigued me. I preferred the sea. The open ocean was my companion.

Pulling my phone from my breast pocket, I dialed Ashan. "Hey, let Sergei and Roman know I am here; all seems calm. I will let you know once the deal is sealed."

"You sure I couldn't come along? I can still come if you want me there?" Ashan inquired.

"It's just signing a contract. I don't need you to hold my hand. I am certain I can do this by myself. Remember, I have already spoken to the woman, and the deal has been prepared. Stop worrying, and let me get this done."

Ashan sighed before he hung up. I could never understand why he always felt the need to accompany me everywhere. But, then again, he had always looked out for me from a young age.

He may be younger than me, but he has always had a more mature attitude. Now, I was spreading my wings, which maybe scared him a little. I smiled at my reflection in the glass door as I considered this.

Entering the building, I walked to the elevator. The floor tiles were lovely marble, which contradicted the silver shine of elevator doors perfectly. I pressed the button, but the light didn't blink or move. It appeared to be stuck on the second floor.

Walking up the stairs to the real estate company's office that listed the beachfront property, I couldn't shake this feeling. I glanced back several times as I ascended. Ashan was always going on about listening to the small voice. But before now, I have never been one to listen.

I loved the adrenaline from taking risks. Ashan always complained I was reckless, even though I only took chances on things I knew I could handle. He never took chances. He had always been the cautious one. Today, however, I would proceed with caution as it felt like something was crawling under my skin.

The family needed this piece of land, and nothing would stand in our way. The agent said she would keep it for us until this morning when I spoke to her last week. We agreed on price, terms, and transfer. Now, it was simply down to getting the paperwork done.

On the second-floor landing, I noticed two men standing at the elevator door, holding it open. That's why it wouldn't work. Passing them, I turned up the short passage and walked to the office door. They nodded in greeting, but my senses told me to keep an eye on them.

They were definitely out of place at the estate agent's office. Plus, the bulges on the sides of their jackets indicated weapons. Maybe the owner of the property was here, I thought.

Glancing back, I knocked on the frosted glass door. There were voices inside, but I couldn't make out what they were saying. I pulled the handle down and slowly pushed the door open.

Towards the back of the room was a large oak desk with two chairs before it on my side and one behind it. To the left, I noticed two men, most likely guards, also armed. They were standing with their hands at

Hostage of the Bratva

Forced Marriage Mafia Romance

Morozov Bratva Book 10

Lexi Asher

CONTENTS

their sides. On the right were two more, and in the chairs on this side of the desk sat two men with their backs to me.

The chair behind the desk was occupied by a lovely young woman with long black hair. Yet, from her expression, she looked like she could be in a ghost house or on a scary rollercoaster as her face seemed colorless.

Her green eyes were wide, and her arms folded across her chest. She didn't smile or greet me as I entered the room. The large open window behind her brought in a nice cool breeze and stirred the locks of hair hanging over her shoulders.

I might have asked her out for a drink if I wasn't here for business. Her big breasts were nicely displayed by her extremely tight cream-colored V-neck top. I had to admit big breasts had always been one of my downfalls, as I simply couldn't resist them.

As the door closed behind me, I felt a stiffening in my spine as my senses lit up. I realized I had just walked into a situation. The men in the room were not the owners. Something else was going on.

"Morning," I said calmly. "I'm sorry, I thought we had a meeting," I looked at my watch to make sure I had the time right. "I'm Luder; we spoke on Friday," I said as I walked to the desk and held out my hand to her.

She glanced up at me and then at the two men across from her. "Yes, I'm sorry, the property is no longer available." She replied softly. "You have to leave as I am busy. Sorry for not letting you know earlier."

I scanned the room, and the two men seated at my side. The older man looked slightly familiar. But, in that instant, I couldn't recall where I had seen him before.

"Mathieu," the older man spoke in a deep tone as he tapped the younger man's arm.

"Yes, boss," Mathieu said as he rose from his chair.

He loosened the button and pulled back his dark blue suit jacket as he placed his right hand on the butt of his gun. "The lady asked you to leave. Now leave." He spat as he stepped closer.

Looking over his shoulder at the older man, it dawned on me. He was Domique Anchony of the Anchony Bratva. They were surely here to take the property we wanted. This wasn't going to end well. I felt my stomach churning as my automatic response kicked in.

7

Glancing at the other men, I noticed they were all ready to take me out. I couldn't let this happen, as it would start a war. Not that a war was uncommon, but me dead wasn't ideal. As I stepped back carefully, I undid my jacket button and crossed my hand up to my Glocks. Looking at the woman behind the desk, I considered jumping out the open window behind her.

"I'm sorry," I said as I straightened out. "We had already paid over the deposit." I stood still in the middle of the floor, waiting for them to make the first move. Ashan would have said my odds were not good, seeing as they were six, and I should call for backup. Yet, there was no time or way that they would allow me to make a call.

I grinned at Mathieu as he looked back to Anchony for approval. Anchony stared at me as if trying to burn me with his eyes. But obviously, that didn't work; he was assessing my threat. He nodded at Mathieu, and I knew that was my cue.

Out the side of my eye, I caught the sun's rays reflecting off the barrel of a gun. Ducking, I turned as and pulled the Glocks from their holsters. I took the first shot as I wasn't waiting for an invitation. The noise blew through the room with a mighty force. Blood splattered the once nice cream-colored wall behind him as the guard dropped. I felt a bullet blowing past my ear. Shifting, I fired again, I hit the other guard solidly in the chest, and he went down as I turned.

The window was no longer an option, and the young woman was hiding under her desk, which was a good option for her. I realized I would have to move back the way I came in. "Anchony, you know this wasn't needed." I spat as I ducked down and shot at the two other guards while moving for the door. I didn't have time to make sure they went down as I needed to get out.

Anchony rose from his chair and turned to face me. "You know you're not getting out of here alive," he said, smirking as he raised his gun. I felt a burning sting as I slid backward through the door. The other two men who were at the elevator earlier were gone. With no time to waste, I couldn't worry about them right now. I headed for the stairs as I could not take a chance on them being in the elevator.

Looking down at my arm, a trick of blood congealed through my jacket just below my shoulder. Jumping the last three steps, I kneeled as my feet hit the ground. To my left and the way out stood three more guards. I was sure it must be the two from the elevator, but I didn't know where the other one came from.

Turning right, I quickly stepped through another frosted glass door. The room was filled with women in skimpy sportswear exercising. Towards the back, I noticed another glass door leading to the sidewalk. I was about halfway across the room when I heard Mathieu screaming for the women to get out of the way.

Glancing back, I knew there was only one way out. Holstering my one gun, I grabbed the woman next to me. As I turned, I held her before me as a shield. Walking backward, I kept the gun to her head.

Mathieu suddenly tucked away his gun, which was a bit confusing. Then I noticed a flicker of fear in his eyes, which I couldn't quite understand either, but it wasn't important. I needed to get away and would do what had to be done.

"Back off, Mathieu," I shouted as I pulled her out the door with me onto the sidewalk.

"You have nowhere to go," he replied, stepping out and raising his hands. "Just let her go, and we can talk about it."

Glancing over my shoulder, I saw two guards coming closer from behind. "Don't shoot," Mathieu called to them as I turned by my car and moved to the driver's side.

"You don't want to talk, just be honest," I shouted back.

"Get the key from my pants pocket, honey," I whispered to the woman. She was shaking but searched my pants pocket and pulled out the key. As her hands searched my pockets, I felt my insides making a quick turn. Not now, I thought, but it was instinct.

"Now press the button," I whispered into her ear. Her touch, mixing with my adrenaline levels, sent a surge of electricity through my veins. This was new but felt good, it was a sensation I would like to follow up on once we got out of here.

I heard the lock snap and the engine turn on, "Open the door and get in." I said as we stepped back slightly. She opened the door but pushed back when I tried to force her inside. "I will shoot you," I said, pushing her forward harder. I felt my dick starting to throb, and for a second, I was a little distracted. Pushing her head down, I forced her in.

As she plummeted into the car, I saw Mathieu pull his gun again. Taking a wild shot, I jumped into the car with her. Mathieu grabbed his chest as we sped off. I was grateful for the bulletproof windows as the bullets coming our way simply got stuck or fell to the ground.

I never considered the need for child locks fitted to all the doors of my car. But now I understood why Ashan had insisted. It was a handy thing to have as I noticed her trying to open the door. The woman looked back, with tears streaking down her cheeks as we drove out of sight.

Taking a couple of quick turns and heading up and down some roads, I ensured we weren't being followed. Not that I had seen them chasing after us. They were focused on Mathieu. But Ashan always cautioned that one could never be too careful. I glanced at the woman and noticed she had pushed herself up against the door.

She was short with a thin middle. But her breasts were surely the thing most men noticed first. I felt my temperature rise as I headed towards Sergei's warehouse. Her blond hair, which had come loose in the struggle, was tied into an updo above her head. Strands of golden silk fell down her shoulders and back. She was alluring even though she wasn't the kind of woman I would consider twice if I met her on the street.

She pushed some golden locks back from her face that were lying over her breasts. I couldn't help the direction my mind suddenly took. I shook my head as we pulled up behind the warehouse. I slowed but didn't stop. No, I must let her go, I tried convincing myself as my mind flooded with images of another nature.

My mind took some crazy turns as it headed down its own path. I imagined having her back at the yacht. She wasn't wearing much, only some black lacy lingerie. Smiling to myself, I shook my head.

I drove on, and pulled into a dark alley not too far away, now parking the car. Turning the engine off, I turned in my seat and looked at her. She didn't move, she sat frozen as I studied her.

Her face had a perfect, sleek contour with luscious lips and big hazel eyes, complimenting her beauty. The long blond strands of silk ran down her back, touching her amazingly firm ass. Moving back up, her middle appeared quite slim for the ample breasts she proudly displayed.

My fingers tingled as my desire for her rose within. Her outfit hugged her so tightly that every curve was visible. She became a distraction, but it was one I liked. Maybe I would hang on to her for just a bit longer.

Chapter 2 - Skyler

Why was he just sitting there staring? My day started out so well. I spent the morning in the park with Bunny, my Husky. After lunch, I should have returned home instead of going to the yoga studio. Then I wouldn't be in this mess. I didn't know what this man wanted, but he shot my brother and kidnapped me.

Driving away and not being able to go to my brother's side felt like a tight band wrapped around my heart. For a moment, as we drove off, I thought I was going to die. I focused on the area outside, trying to regain my strength and see where he was heading.

Thinking back to his tight grasp around my waist, I wondered why it caused a slight tingling feeling to course through my body. I had never in my life felt so scared. But his essence still lingered in my nostrils, causing my mind to wander.

I shifted as he stopped the car and turned to me. Glancing out the window, I felt his eyes scanning me. But I dared not look at him; I wasn't sure if I would be able to control this sudden urge to have him in me. What was happening to my mind?

This was not like me. He wasn't even my type. I racked my mind, trying to figure out why my body was sending all these signals that didn't belong. I didn't know who he was or what would happen to me. But a man with a gun who isn't scared to use it was surely not a good man.

Maybe if we get out, I could make a run for it. After all, I was in flats, and running wouldn't be an issue. No, I told myself, he would just shoot me in the back. I let out a small scream and shook slightly as he touched my shoulder.

"I'm sorry," he said in a calm, deep voice as he sat back again, studying me.

I lowered my gaze and noticed he had placed his gun back in the holster. His suit complimented his build, as I could see it fit him like a glove. Raising my head slowly, I couldn't resist taking in his features.

His shirt was tucked solidly into his pants. I felt sure there wasn't an inch of fat to be found on his body as I noticed his flat stomach and firm chest. His suit jacket stretched tight over his arms, which seemed to bulge out, trying to escape their confines. There was some blood on one sleeve.

Following his prominent jawline, I observed his hair; even though it was cut military style, it looked like soft chocolate. I observed myself staring, and then he moved, and our eyes met. My stomach made a knot as my breath left me, and my lungs felt like they were filled with burning coal.

His one eye was a light sky blue, and the other appeared like a shiny gold ball. This was a scary combination but also intriguing. The rest of his face was clean-shaven, and his dark-tanned skin appeared smooth and soft.

"What do you want?" I inquired lightly, turning my gaze back to the alley.

"I just want to make sure we are safe, then I'll take you wherever you want, okay?" His voice was soothing, like a warm friend's embrace, and I felt myself being pulled.

I didn't answer but gave him a nod as I glanced back at him again. After what felt like a year's silence, he got out of the car. I heard the lock as he closed it and knew I couldn't even try running. I was stuck in his car and could only hope he was a man of his word.

He stood outside, making a call. I could not hear him, but I could see he wasn't pleased. He turned his back toward me as he waved his hand in the air while talking. He placed the phone back in his jacket and slammed his fists onto the car's hood.

I shifted in my seat out of fear but kept my scream in this time. He walked around to my side and opened the door, holding out his hand to me. Warily, I took it and got out. He held me by my upper arm in a tight grip as we walked out of the alley and across the road to a warehouse.

"Please," I begged. "Please let me go, I won't say anything to anyone, I promise."

He unlocked a steel door and forced me inside without a word. The building was basically empty. Towards the back, there seemed to be an office or a small room. There were a couple of large barrels, some boxes, a table, and a chair in the other corner. But other than that, the place was bare.

He pulled me toward the room at the back. Glancing around at the closed door, I wished I had tried running. I was sure being dead would have been a better option. Even though I had no idea what his plans with me were, I would rather have taken the bullet.

He shot my brother, so why not me too, my mind kept telling me. No, he said he would let me go. I had to hold on to hope, I convinced myself. My feet filled with lead as he dragged me across the floor. My lungs felt like they were about to give up on me as I unexpectedly gasped for air.

I didn't want to die, not here, not this way. "Please, Mr., please, let me go." I tried again as we neared the small room.

He pulled me in and grabbed my other arm, holding me up facing him. "I told you; I will let you go once I know it is safe." His voice was no longer smooth and warm. It was scary and made me cold as a shiver ran down my spine.

Letting go of one arm and turning me back into the room, I noticed a chair in one corner. There was an old desk, and also a couch. He shoved me forward onto the couch. I caught the side and turned, taking a seat. As I sat back, rubbing my arms where he had held me, I wondered if I would get bruises from the tight grip. The couch wasn't the most comfortable and smelled, but it was at least soft.

He took off his jacket and threw it over the chair before rolling up his sleeves. Then he started walking up and down the small room with his hands on his hips as if trying to decide on what to do. His broad chest could now clearly be seen as his shirt stretched across it. After a while, he sat down in the chair. He unbuttoned his shirt and examined his arm before turning his attention back to me.

"Sorry, I didn't mean to hurt you," he said in his calm, deep voice, sending a shiver down my spine. His voice was filled with emotion, and I couldn't place his mood, but he sounded sincere.

I had to do something to convince him I could be trusted. As a modern woman, I knew I had charms that could soften most men, but I wondered if it would work on him. There was only one way to find out, and I had to try.

"It's fine," I answered, smiling softly at him. "May I ask who we are hiding from?" I hoped my voice sounded calm enough to make him feel at ease.

"It's complicated," he replied as he studied me.

Taking that as a good sign, I pressed on. "I'm sorry if I made your day worse."

A gentle smile formed on his lips. "No, it's not you. Sorry I dragged you into this." He looked down at his hands, rubbing them together. I noticed his shoulders relaxing slightly.

"Is there anything I can do to help?" I asked, hoping our conversation would make him see that I was no threat.

He rose and walked over to the couch. "No, just be a little more patient with me, and you will be on your way soon," he said as he sat down next to me.

Being so close, I could smell his sweet aroma. My mind filled with the sweet smell of the ocean on a bright early morning. Closing my eyes for a second, I absorbed this delightful fragrance.

My stomach turned, and I couldn't help but smile up at him. His eyes were filled with a tenderness I could not explain. I found myself wanting to reach out and touch him. Instead, I folded my arms across my chest.

"You need to see a doctor," I said, looking at his shoulder.

"It's just a graze, the bullet didn't go in, so it'll be fine." He responded calmly.

"So, what is this place?" I asked, hoping not to sound too inquisitive. I stood and walked to the chair, looking out through the big window.

"It's my cousin's warehouse, but it isn't being used at the moment." I heard him walking closer as he spoke and turned to find him standing right behind me. I was staring right into his broad chest.

I gasped as my heart suddenly leaped. I tried to step back but found myself up against the chair. I slowly lifted my head from his chest to his chin and up. His lips were slightly parted as he smiled down at me. I found myself wanting him to kiss me, wanting to know how tender those lips were.

Shaking my head slightly, I tried to rid my mind of these devious thoughts as our eyes locked. I was sure that it was only the fear mixed with adrenaline that was causing so much havoc in my mind and body. I needed to get out, but there was nowhere to go with him here.

My breathing felt constricted, and I abruptly sensed a warm glow rising. He was turning me on. I knew this could never work but the heat from within was assisting me to stay calm.

Chapter 3 - Luder

Standing so close to her, looking down into her big hazelnut eyes, the hair on my neck rose with my temperature. Her eyes were so prominent compared to her slim face and luscious lips. An intense desire invaded me, and I wanted her more and more as we talked.

Watching her move, walking from the couch to the chair, her exercise pants hugging her firm ass, I couldn't help but be filled with desire. Even though she had a tiny middle, her breasts surely made up for that. Staring down at them from this angle sent a tingling through my fingers.

The longing to touch her grew. I knew I had to step back, but my feet were frozen.

I only thought about getting out earlier, but now, I wanted more from her than a way out. Even though I knew this could all just be due to the adrenaline and rush from the escape. I felt chemistry between us. I couldn't be sure if her sudden change was due to fear or if she was attracted to me.

But I wasn't going to complain. After all, I will never see her again, so what harm could a bit of play do? It would, however, ease the tension that currently filled every muscle.

"May I ask your name?" I asked, looking into her eyes while I carefully caressed her cheek.

She didn't flinch or pull back and smiled as she spoke. I couldn't take my eyes off her lips. "Skyler, and yours?"

"Luder," I replied without hesitation. I wondered how my name would sound coming from her lips but pushed the thought out quickly.

"Why did you shoot that man?" she asked in a barely audible voice, glancing away for a second.

I rubbed my head. "He was going to shoot me, but that's not important, is it?"

"I guess not," she replied, pulling her mouth to one side. "Do you think he's dead?"

I shook my head, "No, I'm sure he's not." She was trying to distract me but had caught my attention. She was standing relaxed against the chair, gazing up at me.

My mind was racing through all the scenarios, and I didn't want to get distracted. Why was she asking so many questions? I wanted to concentrate on where I would pin her. The chair, the couch, or the table. I was still trying to formulate the next step when she placed her hands on my abs.

"Sorry," she said as she gently pushed me backward. "I think I need to sit down. I'm feeling a little dizzy."

Stepping back, I allowed her to move past me to the couch. My skin was burning where her hands touched, and my senses growled. I felt movement in my pants as the beast within started to wake.

Turning my head, I watched her sway her firm ass as she moved back to the couch. It was time, the beast within screamed. Stepping up behind her, I grabbed her hips and pulled her tightly against me. She froze in my grip as our bodies touched.

My cock was hard and ready, and I was sure she could feel it pumping against her ass. I couldn't simply take her, though. I had to be sure. Leaning closer, I whispered in her ear. "Would you like to have some fun hunny?"

She didn't move but lifted her head and glanced at me. "I might be interested." She replied softly.

I could hear her breathing slightly change as I moved my hands up her sides and took hold of the sides of her top. Slowly, I started moving my hands further up her sides, pulling her top with. She didn't resist as her top made its way up and over her head. At that moment, I knew she also wanted to play.

Her arms moved up as I got to her shoulders, and she allowed me to pull her top up and off. Her skin was hot, smooth, and smelled like roses. I caressed the outside of her arms as my hands made their way back to her sides. She shook lightly as I made tender lines onto her belly and up to her bra.

She gasped as I pushed her bra up with my fingers, cupping her breasts firmly. Her hands instantly came up and covered mine. Her breathing was raspy, and she laid her head back against my chest as she spoke.

"I don't think," she took a deep breath. "I don't want anything serious." She said as I kissed her shoulder.

"Neither do I," I whispered, squeezing her breasts lightly. "Just some fun before we go our separate ways."

Pulling her bra up, she lifted her arms again so I could remove it. I Had to move her long blond hair over her one shoulder as it was tangling in her bra. She giggled slightly as I fumbled with the bra. This made me want her even more. She was a delicate flower ripe for picking.

Placing my hands back on her hips, I kissed her neck and felt her shiver in my grip. I laid a couple of kisses down her back as I turned her towards the table. Gently, I pushed her forward.

She didn't resist, she walked willingly. I was sure that all the events of the day had also impacted her emotions. With so much tension between us, what else was there to do? As we reached the table, she placed her hands against the side. Glancing over her shoulder, I noticed a flicker of fear cross her face.

"Luder," she said softly.

"Yes,"

"I'm not looking for something long-term." She took a deep breath. "Usually, I do not just allow any man to touch me." She added before facing the table again.

"Understood, I didn't intend for this, but I feel the same," I replied, kissing her neck. Knowing she felt the same gave me more reason to fuck her. I needed to release the beast, she was here and willing, so I was game.

Family was everything at this stage in my life, and we had important things to take care of. I didn't have time for girls and their needs. All I wanted was some fun. I turned her to face me. Gripping her hips, I placed her on the table and moved in between her legs.

Her luscious lips were parted ever so slightly, and I felt my hunger growing. I leaned in and kissed her hard. Her lips parted, and I drove my tongue into her inviting mouth. She tasted so sweet, my veins felt like they were filling with fire as I forcefully pulled her to the edge.

She gasped, and I pulled back an inch. Skyler's fingers fumbled at the buttons on my shirt. As she got the last ones, she pushed the shirt back over my shoulder, and I let it drop to the floor. Her hands moved across my chest, sending all the right signals to my brain. I felt my dick pumping in my pants.

"Luder," she breathed out as I lowered her to the table and placed tender kisses down her neck.

I glanced up at her smiling face. Her blond hair spread around her like the sun. She was a stunning woman.

"Yes," I answered as I moved to her breasts. But her voice disappeared as I gently sucked her nipple. Leaving a trail of kisses down her stomach, I step out of my pants. She quivered as I went moaning softly. Moving in for the taking, I rise and step forward, pulling her down to me.

An hour later, we both sat on the couch, out of breath, hot and sweaty. Her head was lying against my chest as we struggled to regain composure.

"Let's get dressed, then I can drop you off," I said as I stood and pulled my pants on.

Without a word, she rose and got dressed. We walked back out to the car, and I opened the door for her. Skyler smiled as she got in.

I walked around and got in. "Where to?" I asked as I started the car.

"You can just drop me where you took me from," Skyler said, still smiling.

"Well, I can drop you close I suppose, but not at the door. Will that work?"

Skyler nodded and then turned to look out the window. I drove back the way I came and stopped two blocks from the office building.

"Are you sure? I could take you home," I said as she opened the door.

"Thanks, I'm fine here," Skyler commented as she got out and shut the door.

I rolled down the window and looked at her as she stood momentarily. Turning back, she leaned into the window.

"Keep well, Luder, and stay safe." She said before turning and walking up the road.

I watched her until she entered the office building just to ensure she returned safely. Once she was out of sight, I drove off to meet with Ashan. We were having pizza on my yacht. He was to bring the pizza, and I would supply the drinks. We will meet with Sergey and Roman tomorrow to discuss the property and our next move.

When I arrived at the docks, Ashan was already waiting. I parked my car and joined him on the deck of my yacht.

"So," he asked in his usual inquiring tone. "Where have you been all afternoon?"

I smiled as I thought of the activities that followed the meeting. I entered the cabin and opened the bottle of vodka on the table. Grabbing two glasses, I rejoined Ashan on the deck.

"I have been waiting for things to settle, as Roman suggested." I hoped my voice and smile didn't betray me as I spoke.

But Ashan just shook his head. I was surely in the clear and didn't need to go into details with him. This was one time I didn't feel like sharing with him. I poured each of us a glass and handed him one before sitting down.

Ashan patted me on the shoulder as he usually does when things go wrong. "We'll get it sorted." He added in his chipper voice. "But there is something you're not saying, brother."

I grinned at him and shook my head. We ate in silence and enjoyed two more glasses of vodka before he headed out. Once he was gone, I sat staring at the stars in the sky, thinking of the afternoon activities with Skyler.

She was special, but now wasn't the time to try to form a normal life.

Chapter 4 - Skyler

As I stretched out on my bed, my legs cramped. I smiled, thinking back to yesterday. If it wasn't for my sore butt and aching body, I could have sworn it was all just a dream. As I stared at the ceiling, Bunny jumped up on the bed to greet me with a big whoof and a wagging tail.

"Down, boy, I will take you out in a minute," I told him as I got out of bed. After opening the curtains, and a quick shower, I felt refreshed and ready for the day.

Bunny barked and turned in circles as I picked up his leash. "Yes, yes, just a minute boy." As I bent down to put the collar around him and clip the leach, I felt my hamstrings pulling.

No time for stretching now as Bunny may make a mess indoors, I would have to do it when I got back. I opened the door and headed outside with Bunny. The fresh morning air was cool and welcoming.

Once Bunny had done his thing, we headed back. I had to pack a basket before going to the park. This is our usual Saturday routine. After I got back Yesterday, I called Mathieu to find out if he was seriously injured.

I was relieved to find out it was only a scrape, even though it looked serious. Asking about the man, he claimed he didn't know him and was very upset that he had taken me. But he was glad I was safe and assured me we could talk today. Obviously, I couldn't tell him everything that happened, I thought as a smile crossed my lips.

We were both safe, and that was all that mattered. I did want to know why Luder thought Mathieu wanted to shoot him, though and would ask him when we got together.

Back inside my small townhouse, I placed a bowl of milk down for Bunny while I brewed some coffee. I made some sandwiches for me and Mathieu, packed a flask of coffee, and added some fruit juice.

For Bunny, I took a bowl, a bottle of water, and his favorite snacks. Now, we were ready to head out. I quickly did a couple of stretches as I didn't want Mathieu to see me all stiff, he may just wonder what I did to get so stiff. Smiling at myself, I took the basket, placed Bunny on his lead, and headed to the park.

It was a quick three-block walk to the park. Arriving, I saw our spot was open under the big oak tree. I placed the basket on the table and let Bunny loose. He instantly ran to two other dogs that were his friends. They have been coming here with their owners as long as I can remember, and Bunny loved being with them.

As I headed in their direction, Mathieu came in through the big gate. He waved at me, and I waited for him.

"I am so glad you are okay," I said as we hugged.

"Yes, and you. You are okay?" he asked, pushing me back and looking me over.

I laughed at him, he always got overly worried about me. It got worse once our mother died. But I knew he cared deeply.

I waved at Sara and Matt as they came over. After quickly greeting and catching up on all the news about their two Labradors, Mathieu and I returned to our table. Bunny came tail-wagging to greet my brother before returning to the other dogs.

"So," Mathieu said as he sat down.

"So what?" I asked, handing him a cup of coffee from the flask. The wind blew the morning's cool breeze into the park, and I felt a chill run down my spine. We had to close our cups with our hands as it brought along a couple of leaves as well.

"Tell me what happened after that man drove off with you, is what," Mathieu said. He sounded upset as he spoke, but I couldn't be sure as he was staring off to the side.

"Nothing," I replied, half irritated. "I'm fine. We drove around for a bit, and then he let me go. His beef was with you, not me." I finished placing my hands on my hips.

Mathieu's eyes narrowed as he studied my face. "I had no problem with him except that he took you. Why would you say something like that?"

Picking up my cup, I took a sip before looking him in the eye. "He said you wanted to shoot him."

"Me," Mathieu said as he chuckled, "I wouldn't shoot anyone, you know me."

"Yes, and I told him that."

Mathieu jumped to his feet, spitting out the sip of coffee he took right before I spoke. "You what?" he said in disbelief.

"Yes, I told him you wouldn't shoot him or anyone else. You weren't that kind of person." As I spoke, I noticed Mathieu's face turning white. "Sit down," I said, standing up and walking around to him.

I gently tapped him on the back as he coughed. "You wouldn't be shooting people, would you?" I asked, wondering why he reacted so strangely.

"No, no, I wouldn't." He answered as he sat back down. "What did he say when you told him that?"

Waving my hand in the air, I replied. "Nothing, he just nodded and then let me go." I felt a grin touching my lips as my mind returned to the nontalking parts, and I had to look away so my brother wouldn't see.

"Oh, yes, remember the dog they rescued from the pipe close to the beach last week," I said, changing the subject.

"Yes, the big German Shepard that was trapped. Did he make it?" he asked, smiling at me.

"Yes, he did, he had to get an operation on his back leg, though. But he will make it." I replied, grinning now that I had a reason to grin without having to hide my guilt.

"You do a lot of good, you know," Mathieu said as Bunny ran around. "Saving animals is not an easy task."

I nodded and took out our sandwiches. Mathieu took hold of my hand as I handed him one. "You know I'm proud of you, and Mother would also have been."

"Yes, I know," I replied, wiping the lonely tear running down my cheek.

After lunch, Mathieu said his goodbyes to me and Bunny, and we headed home. He had a business meeting, and I needed to visit the shelter. But, first, Bunny had to go home.

I brushed Bunny out and made sure his food and water bowls were full before going to the shelter. As I filled the animal's food and water bowls, my mind kept wandering back to Luder. His hands were so soft, warm, and affectionate. Closing my eyes, I liked my lips, remembering his hard kisses.

It was one encounter I was going to remember for the rest of my life, I thought as I finished my rounds. The sex was like nothing I had experienced before. I shook my head to clear my mind. Even though it was the most amazing sex ever, I didn't want to get serious at the moment.

I wanted to build my life, finish my animal courses, and start my own shelter. Maybe then, I would consider finding the right man. Everything about Luder was wrong, it would never work, I convinced myself as I locked up.

Anyway, I told myself as I took an Uber home. I didn't even know who he was, and he didn't know who I was. Yet, he could probably find out if he wanted to. I smiled at my thoughts. "No, you don't need trouble in your life," I whispered to myself as the driver pulled up to my house.

"Excuse me," the driver said, glancing back at me.

"No, nothing, sorry, thanks," I replied, paying him.

Bunny was waiting at the door when I returned, and after a quick walk for him to do his business, I took a long soaking bubble bath. My muscles were still sore, but I could still feel his touch when I closed my eyes. His fingers were magic, but oh my, his tongue. I giggled as my mind took my body through all that he did.

I got into bed, still feeling giddy, but was glad I didn't know who he was. We would never work. Bunny joined me on the bed as I fell asleep, my mind still toying with his touch.

Chapter 5 - Luder

Staring at the ceiling, I found myself wondering what Skyler was doing. The sun had not yet appeared, and I supposed she would be sleeping. Not everyone was an early riser like me. I had to admit that even though she was not the type of woman I usually hung out with, the sex was great. She was a firecracker.

"It could be due to the adrenalin rush of the earlier events, but it was good," I told the ceiling. I still felt relaxed even with everything going on. Sitting up, I glanced out the large window at the calm outside. The ocean was peaceful, and the early morning breeze was cool.

I pulled on my pants, shirt, and shoes. Grabbing my jacket, I headed out. On my way to Roman's house, I stopped at the beach for a black coffee and to admire the sunrise.

"It may still turn out to be a hot day," I said to the barista as he handed me my cup. He simply nodded and went about his business. I breathed in deeply, allowing the ocean air to fill my lungs, then drank my coffee as my mind strolled back to her naked body displayed on the old table.

Chucking the empty cup, I returned to my car, shaking my head. Upon my appearance at Roman's place, I was surprised to see everyone had already arrived. Here, I thought I would be the first. Karine escorted me through to the garden, where the men waited for breakfast.

After a quick greeting, I took my place at the table. Roman poured me a cup of coffee and I sat listening to Roman and Sergey talking about the plans for the next shipment arriving in a week.

There was time for every discussion, and I would have my turn after breakfast. For now, I sat back and enjoyed the coffee and the view. Karine and Irina brought out our plates and placed them on the table.

It looked delicious and smelled even better. After we ate, and the women collected the plates, we could get down to why I was there.

"So then, Luder, tell us what went down yesterday. We thought the property was all set?" Roman inquired as he poured another round of coffee.

"It was," I replied as I shook my head. "I don't know what happened over the weekend. But when I arrived, Domique Anchony was there with his men."

"Domique?" Sergey asked, raising his one eyebrow. "What on earth could they want with that land?"

"I don't know," I replied. "They weren't too friendly to see me, though, and I had to get out. I haven't had time yet to go back to the agent to find out what happened. But…"

"No, no," Roman said as he rose. "No, we will send someone else to find out. They have seen you and will be waiting."

"They did tell me to let you know that the property was no longer for sale," I added as we all rose and followed Roman to the edge of the garden.

"It is time to make a stand, brother," Sergey added as we looked out over the ocean. "They need to know who they are messing with, don't you think?"

Roman turned and faced us. "Yes, I also think it is time we spoke to Ivan." Roman rubbed his stubbled chin as he looked toward the house. "How many did you say were there?" he asked.

"Well, I noticed two men as I headed inside the office. I saw five plus Domique. I shot some before realizing I was outgunned and had to leave. There may have been more, though."

"We need to find out where they are holding up, and Ivan might have details on this. I'll give him a call," Roman said as he headed inside.

It wasn't long before Roman came back out. "Let's go, Ivan is waiting for us." He called from the doorway.

The trip to Ivan's club was quick, and we were greeted with open arms as usual. We headed through the club to his office at the back for a sit-down.

"Right," Ivan said as we took our places. "I've heard that they have a great deal of property on the upper side and some close to the agency where Luder had his encounter with them."

"I suggest we check it out and see which one is active. They won't be at all of them at once." Roman replied.

"Yes, we need to hit them where it will have the most impact," Sergey added.

Ivan rose and poured each of us a drink. "I'll take my men to the two upper side locations." He said as he handed us a glass and sat back down.

"We'll check out those close to the agency with Luder, Ashan, and our men," Roman added.

"Salute," Ivan said, holding up his glass.

We all did the same, and once we finished our drinks, we headed out. Sergey and Roman drove up front, and I followed them with Ashan. Roman slowed down about two blocks from the agency building. We parked beside him to find out why he was stopping.

"We'll sit on the house here on the corner. You two go past and check out the warehouse six blocks up from the agency." Roman said, leaning slightly out of his window.

"Right, see you in about four hours," Ashan replied before we drove off.

As we passed the building and the studio, I couldn't help but try and see inside. My mind abruptly wandered to Skyler. Would she be attending her usual class, or would she be staying clear for a while I thought to myself.

"You looking for something?" Ashan asked as we passed and turned up the next street.

"No," I replied quickly, maybe a bit too quickly, as Ashan's expression changed.

"What happened yesterday? Why do I get the feeling you're not telling me everything?" he inquired as his eyebrows rose.

I couldn't keep the grin from forming on my lips, and for a moment, I didn't even answer him. My mind was invaded by thoughts of her.

Feeling her body squirm, tasting her succulent lips, her breasts. I shook my head, trying to clear the attacking images as I felt the beast start to wake. This was not the time for things such as this.

"There is something you're not telling me, Luder," Ashan said as he tapped my shoulder. "Come on, spill it."

Glancing over at him, I gave Ashan a soft smile. "Somethings are just private, bro," I said before looking back out the window.

Ashan laughed, "So, you weren't alone at the warehouse then?" he asked in an overly chipper voice.

"No," I started and then saw the place we were looking for. "There," I said, pointing to a big brown building about halfway up the block. "That's the place."

"This discussion isn't over; we'll continue it later," Ashan said as he pulled up to the curb on the opposite side.

"Yeah, yeah," I said, grinning at him.

We sat in the same place for about half an hour. Then we drove around two blocks and came down the other street and parked there. A dark blue van pulled into the side entrance as we were about to drive around again. We took down the registration and drove around for ten minutes or so before returning.

Once we returned, we stopped on the other side again. But this time, we parked closer to the warehouse. Ashan got out and walked up to the end of the block. He stood there for a bit, scanning the area, and then came back.

"Any movement?" I inquired as he got back in the car.

"It looks like they are loading some boxes on the side." He replied as he started the car. "This is an active warehouse. I think we should get coffee and come back in about twenty minutes or so."

"Good idea," I said as he pulled away. "I saw this little coffee place next to the building where the agency is, maybe we could stop there. It's not too far."

Ashan looked at me but parked before the door of the coffee shop and got out. "You wait here, we don't want to take a chance of someone recognizing you. I'll grab the coffee."

I nodded as he turned and headed inside. The sun was reflecting off the yoga studio windows, and I couldn't see inside. Glancing at the coffee shop door, I got out and walked to the front of the car.

All I wanted was to see if she was there. There was movement inside, but I could still not make out any of the women.

"Hey, get back in the car. Do you want them to see you?" Ashan roared at me as he came out.

"Okay, okay," I said with my hands up in the air. "I was just looking to see if I could spot any of the guards from yesterday. Don't get your knickers in a twist."

We drank our coffee first before heading back to the warehouse. The van was gone when we returned. We sat on one corner and then another corner for about an hour in total again. This time, there was no movement.

We returned after grabbing sandwiches for lunch from another shop around the corner. This time, two black sedans were parked at the gate on the front side. After about twenty minutes, I saw Mathieu coming out and getting into one of the cars.

"That's him," I said, pointing. "That's Mathieu, Domique's right-hand man."

"Okay, so we know we are at the right place then. Time to head back and share what we know." Ashan said as he started the engine.

Ashan let Roman know we were headed back to Ivan's club. As we passed the Office building and the Yoga studio again, I couldn't help but look back. Skyler was still lingering in my mind. I couldn't rid myself of the lightning streaming through my veins whenever I thought of her.

I knew I had to focus, but my mind wouldn't let go. I smiled out the window as we drove. The images in my mind were still so fresh. I could almost still smell her sweetness.

Roman and Sergey were waiting as we pulled up to the side of Ivan's club. I shook my head and wiped the silly smile from my lips before getting out. I couldn't afford to have them notice something was up.

Entering Ivan's office, we took our places as before. "Right," Ivan started. "Now that we know which of the places are active, we can put lookouts there."

Ivan pushed his hand through his graying hair before continuing. "Luder," I shook my head in acknowledgment as he looked at me. "You call and make another appointment with the broker in about six weeks if convenient for her. Make sure she knows that this time, there will be no interference."

"Sure thing, Ivan," I replied.

"We will settle business, and then all go together to ensure we get this sale done." He finished.

Everyone agreed with each other before we headed out. We would meet back at the club every day to monitor the progress and ensure we had men where they would do the most damage when the time came. Ashan came back with me to my yacht, as most of his weapons were also stored with me.

We ensured they were all cleaned and loaded, ready for action. We packed bags for a long time and stored them safely for when we needed them. While we were doing our preparation, he kept bugging me about my behavior earlier. But I kept my silence.

Skyler wasn't something I was ready to talk about. After all, there was nothing to talk about. It was a one-time fling. Yes, my mind wouldn't let go at the moment, but in time, I thought she would just be another one.

I just couldn't figure out why my mind and body kept going back. What about her was so strong that I had this deep desire for her?

Once we were packed and everything was ready for tomorrow, we headed out for pizza and some beers. It was late when Ashan dropped me back at the yacht, but there was still enough time to catch some ZZZs.

"I'll meet you at Roman's at dawn," I said as I got out.

"Sure, don't forget anything," Ashan replied before driving off.

The next couple of weeks were going to be busy, but honestly, I enjoyed these times the most.

Sleep eluded me for most of the night as Skyler twirled through my thoughts. When I finally felt sleep creeping in, it was nearing dawn.

Chapter 6 - Skyler

Sitting in the waiting area, I felt my stomach turning. The nausea has been killing me for the last three days. I must have caught some kind of stomach flu. I didn't know how, though. I took my vitamins, ate right, kept fit, and never went out in the cold.

Heck, I didn't even get close to people when I knew they were sick. Not even Mathieu. I haven't been sick in four years, and now everything around me makes me feel ill.

The receptionist came out and called my name. Walking into the doctor's office, I felt my insides turning wildly. I was here yesterday for blood tests and didn't expect any results until tomorrow. But the woman at the front desk called and said the doctor wanted to see me.

Taking a seat, the doctor smiled at me as he spoke. I couldn't believe my ears. My mouth hung open as I listened to the doctor's diagnosis. This couldn't be; how did I let this happen? I felt the tears burning my eyes as reality sunk in.

"Miss," Dr Richards said as he stepped around his table and touched my shoulder. "I take it this was not planned." He took a deep breath as I shook my head. "Are you okay?"

I closed my mouth and swallowed the lump in my throat. "Yes," I whispered. "Yes, I will be fine. Thank you, doctor."

Slowly, I rose from the chair and clutched my purse to my chest as I started for the door. Opening the door, I glanced back. "Thank you again," I said as I stepped out.

My legs felt heavy, as if they were suddenly filled with lead. My heart seemed to have sunken to my stomach and was about to stop working. I took a couple of deep, slow breaths, trying to regain my composure before moving.

The waiting room was full of people, and most of them appeared happy and excited. To me, the room seemed to be closing in. The furniture and walls were floating and turning; my head felt light as my vision blurred.

I felt a hand taking my arm, "Are you okay, miss," a woman asked. I looked to my side, and an elderly woman in a nurse's outfit stood beside me. I nodded to indicate I was fine but knew I wasn't. My whole life had been flipped over. "Maybe you should sit for a moment," she said as we walked forward. "You look a bit pale."

The woman assisted me to a chair, and I sat down. I sunk my head between my hands and bit back the tears. Shortly afterward, the woman came back, bringing me a glass of water. "Here, drink this," she said as she held the glass for me to take.

I took some deep breaths and then a couple of sips. The water tasted sweet, and the turning room started slowing down. Sitting up in the chair, I felt the blood returning to my face and the lump in my throat settling. I emptied the glass and handed it back to the woman standing beside me.

"Thank you," I said as I rose, feeling slightly better. I felt all eyes on me and only wanted to get out.

"Can I call someone for you?" she inquired as I started to walk towards the door.

Glancing back, I lifted my hand as I spoke. "No, thanks, I'm fine."

There was a refreshing, cool breeze outside. I stepped to the curb, took out my phone, and booked an Uber. While I waited for the driver, I inhaled deeply, allowing my lungs to absorb the coolness in the air. By the time the Uber arrived, I was actually feeling much better. Not about my predicament, but most of the sudden nausea and lightheadedness was gone.

The driver didn't bother to ask me any questions, which was welcome. The drive home was quick.

Opening the door, Bunny was there to greet me with a loving bark and wagging tail. "Hi, Bunny," I said as I closed the door and fell to my knees. "What are we going to do with a baby," I said as the tears started streaming down my cheeks. Bunny nudged my side and settled next to me.

For the longest moment, I simply sat on the floor, hugging Bunny and allowing my emotions to run out through my eyes. After a while, the shock started to subdue and was replaced by fear.

I rinsed my face and studied the puffiness around my eyes in the bathroom mirror. "How could you be so stupid," I told my reflection. "It had to be his baby, there has been no one else."

Feeling the lump returning to my throat, I swallowed it down. No, I couldn't let the situation turn me into a baby myself. I was stronger than that. After rinsing my face again, I headed to the kitchen. I put the percolator on for coffee and pulled my laptop closer.

Opening the browser, I sat glaring at the screen, wondering how I would find him with only a name. He drove a fancy car and wore suits, yet he owned a gun and went around shooting people. I typed in his name and ran a local search for bachelors, criminals, and anything tied to those. There was nothing else I could do about the information I had.

While the internet worked on the search, I poured some coffee. Sitting back down, I wondered if there was anything else I shouldn't be taking in now that I was pregnant. Staring at the cup, I decided not to and pushed it to the side.

My screen was filled with articles and profiles of men with the name Luder. It was surprising that it was not such a rare name. I started scouring through the information one page at a time. There were a couple I left open as I felt he might be one of those.

Once I had gone through everything, I returned my attention to the three men left. There was a Luder Pantonio, a Luder Morozov, and one Luder Argustus. The first surname sounded more Italian to me, so I closed the page. The second one sounded more on target than the last one.

I decided to stick to the second one as I felt sure he was Russian, and the surname also sounded Russian. "Bunny," I said as I grabbed a glass of water and poured out the coffee. "I think I've found him."

Sitting back down, I dug in. I looked for anything I could find on the surname Morozov. There was more information than I expected, but nothing concrete. After hours and hours of reading articles and searching all avenues, I came upon something.

This was it. The owner of this club had the same surname, and his cousin owned a warehouse. I was sure it was the one where he held me, as the location on Google seemed about right.

Sure, it had to be his family. I searched more. I could be wrong, and it could only be my need to confront him driving me. There were a couple of other people with the same surname, but I couldn't explain it, this one just fit. After looking up the club, the warehouse, and the owners some more, I found more than I had hoped for.

I pushed the laptop back on the counter as I stood up. "No, no," I exclaimed as I turned and walked to the window. Bunny jumped up from his mat by the couch and came tripling over, whining. I grabbed hold of the windowsill as I stared out.

"This is bad, this is very bad," I said out loud as I swung forward and back, bending down and up while still holding the windowsill. I felt my heart racing as my mind whirled through the information I had uncovered.

"You dumb woman," I spat at my reflection, slapping the window. "You should have known better, he is Bratva!" I yelled. Turning, I faced Bunny; leaning back against the window, I steadied myself. My skin got cold, and then sweat started breaking out as my mind shuffled through the details.

The nausea had returned with the rapid onset of fear upon fear. "In what normal life do things like this happen, Bunny?" I whispered as I lowered myself to the ground and pulled Bunny into my arms.

Seated on the floor against the wall with my legs spread out, holding onto my dog for life, I felt my eyes stinging as the tears started again. My breathing was labored, and I gasped at the air in the room. "Maybe I should just leave this alone. Who knows what will happen if I tell him."

Bunny was licking my leg and pawing at me as if trying to comfort me. "I know, Bunny, I know." I wiped the tears with the back of my hand. "These people are dangerous," I added, taking a deep breath. "But, you know," I said, looking down at his furry face. "They are people."

Taking Bunny's head in my hands, I swallow my tears. "This is not me, no, I am in control of my life," I said as I kissed his head. "Wallowing is for babies, not for me." After I gave Bunny a big hug, he licked my arm. Rising, I was ready to face whatever life threw at me.

I decided, and my mind was made up, I would at least let him know. I took a quick shower, pulled on a pantsuit, and put on some make-up to hide the bags under my eyes, before doing my hair. Stepping out of the bathroom I felt a little more at ease. What was the name of that club, I wondered as I headed to the kitchen.

Pulling the laptop closer I was glad I didn't close it all. I wrote down the club's name, owner, and address. Looking around I made sure I had my phone, wallet, and my handbag. "I'll be back shortly, Bunny," I said, rubbing his head before heading for the door.

Once outside I noticed the day had passed quickly while I wallowed on my kitchen floor. The evening had started crawling in, but it was still light out. The Uber was already waiting at the curb. I told the driver where I wanted to go, and we drove off. I still felt a bit nervous but determined.

As the driver stopped in front of the club, I wondered if I was making a mistake. The door flung open, and a handsome young man held out his hand for me. Well, I thought, it was too late now to turn around. I took his hand and got out.

Walking up to the doors, I noticed the place was quiet. I wasn't sure if this was a good or bad thing. Stopping at the door, I looked around. There were only a handful of people inside. Most were the cleaners and servers. I walked up to the bar where two young men were packing glasses on a shelve.

"Excuse me," I said as I sat down.

"Yes, mam," the one said as he turned and approached me. "We are not quite open, but how can I assist?" he asked in a friendly tone.

"It's fine, I'm not here to drink. I'm looking for Luder Morozov?" I stated, glancing around. I expected the people to all stop what they were doing and look at me. But no one did. I smiled, wondering if I watched too many movies.

"Luder, mam?" the bartender asked.

"Yes, you do know him, don't you?"

The man looked back at the other barman, who had stopped shelving the glasses. "It's fine," he said as he came over. "You finish putting the glasses back. I got this." He appeared older than the first man. He had an aura of authority, and I suspected he might be in charge.

"Hi, I'm Mike," he said, holding out his hand.

"Hi, Mike," I replied as I shook his hand. "Can you tell me where I can find Luder?"

He pushed his hand through his scruffy black hair as he leaned onto the counter. "He's not in right now, but you can wait, or I can give him a message?" he said, grinning.

Turning slightly away from him, I noticed some of the staff whispering. "No, it's fine. I'll wait. Can I sit at the table close to the door?" I asked, pointing to a table in the corner.

"Sure thing, can I get you anything while you wait?" he inquired as I rose.

"No, thanks," I said over my shoulder as I briskly walked to the table. I felt out of place, and the way he was looking at me made my stomach turn.

The table was bolted to the floor, made from what looked like a good solid oak. I wondered why they would bolt them down as I sat in the chair facing the door. I had to admit the place was lovely inside. I would never have thought it to be a Mafia club had I come here before. Not that I knew what a Mafia club would have that a normal club wouldn't.

Even the chairs were bolted down. But I had to admit, they were comfortable. Most of the people had returned to what they were doing, and I felt better not having so many eyes on me. I held my purse in my lap as I studied the décor.

As time started passing, and people started coming in, I wondered how long I would have to wait. After an hour, I walked back to the bar and ordered fruit juice. I had hoped the bartender would be able to give me a time frame, but he couldn't say.

I returned to the table with my juice, hoping it wouldn't take too much longer as I felt a bit hungry. Plus, I had to get back to Bunny, who was alone at home. But I waited as I knew if I left now, I wouldn't be back.

Chapter 7 - Luder

We had monitored and planned everything for the last six weeks. Now, it was time to get the purchase agreement signed. We had made sure that the Anchony Family would be very busy so we could get in and out without any issues.

After tracing some of their shipments, we managed to cause a couple of delays. So, they ought to be busy clearing the mess for the next day or two. Hopefully, this would allow us to move forward with our own business plans.

This time, Roman, Sergey, and Ashan were with me when we pulled into the front of the building. All appeared quiet; there were no signs of anyone or any other cars for that matter. Only one light burned inside on the second floor.

I pressed the buzzer on the door and waited for the clicking sound so we could enter. Heading up the stairs, I felt my stomach making a sudden swirl. Something was off, but I couldn't put my finger on it. It wasn't quite like the first time, so I said nothing.

Maybe it was quiet, but I wasn't too sure about that. We entered the hallway and passed the elevator. Still nothing. My mind was toiling with me, I thought as we entered the agent's office.

There, as before, sat the lovely Miss Jones behind her desk. The large window behind her opened, but the two chairs on this side of the desk were empty. I felt a river of relief wash over me as we walked up to her desk.

"Miss Jones," I said, reaching out across her desk as she stood up. "Finally, we meet in calmer circumstances."

"Luder, I presume," she said as she met my hand halfway. She glanced from me to the others as we shook hands. "Not alone this time, I see," she added before sitting back down.

"This property is too important to have interference like last time." Roman chipped in as he took a seat. "Can we move this along, please?"

"Sure thing," Miss Jones said, handing Roman a folder. "You will see everything is as we discussed." Roman nodded at her. He opened the file and started scanning through the documents. As he finished with each, he handed it to Sergey, who carefully studied them as well.

Once they were done, Roman looked at Sergey for confirmation. Sergey nodded at him. The two had an amazing connection I thought. They always knew what the other was thinking.

"Everything seems in order," Roman said as he placed the file open on the desk and took out his pen.

As he was about to sign, his phone rang. Roman placed the pen down and rose as he took the call. He walked out of the office and stood just outside as he spoke to whoever was calling.

Roman's expression suddenly changed. He hung up and opened the door. "No time, we have to move now." He spat before turning and heading to the elevator. Sergei and Ashan followed swiftly.

"I'm sorry, we will be back, please keep this private," I said to Miss Jones as I rose and sprinted to the elevator. I didn't know what had just happened, but it had to be big for Roman to dismiss this meeting so instantly.

"What's happening, Roman," Sergey asked as we walked into the elevator and watched the doors close.

"That was Ivan. One of the other clubs just received a note warning us to let this sale go. If we don't comply, they will blow up one of the clubs." He spoke through clenched teeth, his fists formed tight at his sides.

"What?" Sergey snapped. "Does Ivan think the threat is credible?"

Ashan glanced at me with raised eyebrows. This was too sudden; how did they know? I wondered if we didn't have a leak somewhere. Yet, this deal was kept extremely silent. Only a handful of people knew. It could only be the agent, she was the only odd ball.

As we pulled around the back of Ivan's club, I noticed a lot of the family were present. Most of the cousins had come to discuss the issue at hand. Cars and guards crowded the private parking area. We joined the family as they entered the club and convened inside the backroom.

"Thanks for coming," Ivan said. "We have to deal with this issue soon. As all of you know, this piece of land is vital. We need it for the access to the ocean it offers. So, the floor is open for suggestions."

After listening to and hearing the suggestions, it was settled. The Anchony family was to be taken out of the game for good. Blood was about to flow through the streets of Miami.

Each member received their orders before leaving. Due to the information, we gathered during the last couple of weeks, it was possible to target all of their places at once. Roman and Sergey got to go back to the house, and they kept an eye on a couple of men.

Ivan and Leo would take two of the clubs while Nikolai, Aleksei, and Yuri took some of the warehouses. Ashan and I were left with the warehouse we had sat on, and our orders were clear, nothing was to be left standing.

We were the last ones to leave. As we waited for the items, we would need to be loaded into our cars, one of the barmen came around back looking for me.

"Mr. Luder," he said grinning as he sprinted toward me and Ashan. "I'm glad I caught you." He added, out of breath as he stopped before us. "There is," he took a deep breath. "There is a lady inside insisting on seeing you today."

I glanced back at the back entrance. "A lady, for me?" I asked, a bit confused. Ashan smiled eerily, pulling his face up on one side as he stepped closer.

"Now, this I have to see," he said, walking past me.

"Wait, Ashan," I said, grabbing him by his jacket. My mind was still trying to consume the barman's words. I have never given any woman my name and surname together. I sure as hell haven't even mentioned the club or any other place to anyone.

"This might be a trap," I said as Ashan turned to me.

Ashan burst out laughing, "A woman coming to look for you is a trap?" he inquired as he pulled away from me. "Now, how could that be, brother?" he questioned.

"I've never given any details to any of the women," I replied shortly.

"She's been here since before we opened. She insisted on waiting." The barman added.

"Now, now, Luder," Ashan prompted as he took my arm and dragged me to the club entrance. "Let's not keep her waiting any longer."

I was sure Ashan had gone insane. He knew me better than this. He knew I would never bring a girl into the picture or give out details about the family and the club. It was impossible that she was here to see me. We had to move, there was business to take care of, I didn't have time for this.

"Let her wait, Ashan," I protested, trying to pry his hand from me. "We have more important things to do brother."

"No, no, a man doesn't let a woman wait. Where's your manners?" he spoke harshly as we moved to the door.

Ashan wouldn't let it go, so I willingly went in to get this sorted so we could leave. Ashan was close on my heels as we entered the club. The barman pointed to a table just inside the door to the left. As my eyes adjusted to the lighting, I froze. Could it be, was that her?

Ashan shoved me forward, almost sending me tumbling to the floor. Stepping forward, she turned and looked at me. It was her. Skyler was sitting there waiting for me. Glancing over my shoulder, I raised my hand and showed Ashan to stop.

"No, Ashan, wait outside," I spoke, giving him a warning glare.

He froze on the spot, knowing better than to pursue me anymore, and stepped back. "I'll get you outside," he said. "Don't take too long, though."

I nodded and turned my attention back to Skyler. My heart was beating at my ribcage, and I felt my blood starting to boil. Pushing my hand through my hair as I stepped up to the table, I wondered why she was there. No, my mind screamed. How did she find you? That was the most important question.

Yes, that was more important as she could actually be part of the enemy, I thought. Thinking back to the getaway, she did seem awfully concerned about Mathieu when I shot him.

"Hello, Skyler," I said as I sat down opposite her, staring into her eyes. There was something different about her, she seemed to be glowing in the dark light of the club. My heart started pounding in its confines, her eyes were filled with a penetrating passion I had not seen before.

Sweat formed in my palms as the beast within wanted more of her. I shifted in my chair, feeling a wave of heat passing over me. Her sweet aroma again filled my lungs, and my mind flashed back to the warehouse. Closing my eyes for a second, I could taste her sensuous lips.

The chemistry we had at that moment was incredible. She was a wild one; shaking my head, I fought to clear the images from my mind. I had to focus. This wasn't the time or place for such things.

It took me six weeks to get her out of my mind, and now she was back. I felt sure I was being punished for something.

"Hi, Luder," she replied softly, her lips moving slowly. "You are a hard man to find, you know." Her voice was laced with a sensuality my body craved.

The smile on my lips vanished as I remembered I needed to know how she found me.

"You weren't supposed to find me at all," I said, straightening up. "May I know how you happen to come upon my connection to this club?" I spoke, clearing my throat. Maybe I was the leak, I wondered. Yet, I was sure I had not said anything to her that could have revealed my identity.

CHAPTER 8 - SKYLER

"Well," I started saying as I glanced around before leaning over the table. I grabbed hold of his dark blue tie, pulling him closer as I continued in a whisper. "That's not important, Luder. I'm just here to let you know that I'm pregnant." I calmly spat the words out and sat back, studying his reaction.

Luder's eyes widened, and his mouth fell open. "You're what?" he replied in a raised voice as he rose from the table. Once the words had left his mouth, he must have realized he was almost screaming. He glanced around. The staff had all stopped what they were busy with and were looking at us.

"Wait, wait a minute," he said as he walked around the table and pulled me up by my arm. "Come with me. We need to talk privately."

The cleaners and waiters preparing before opening the doors whispered between each other. I sensed their cold eyes on me and wondered why I felt like the culprit. After all, I didn't do anything wrong. I simply wanted him to know.

We walked towards the far side of the bar. There was a passage with a sign hanging from the roof. The sign indicated two bathrooms and an office down the hallway. I felt his grip tighten as we moved down the passage.

"Stop," I said, glancing back as I tried to stop by pulling backward. Instinctively, I tried to loosen his grip on my arm as fear of what may come invaded my mind. "It's quiet enough right here; if you want to talk, talk, but I'm not going into a back room with you."

Luder stopped and looked at me. "Really," he said, letting me go and lifting his arms in the air. "What do you think of me?" he asked, leaning in to look me in the eyes. His face told a story of pain and hurt. I actually felt sorry for him but couldn't say why. His change of attitude made me uncomfortable but also gave a tingling sensation down my back.

I didn't comprehend what was happening to me. I rubbed my arm where he held me, I was sure his hold was going to leave a mark. "I don't…" I replied. "What am I supposed to think?" I added as he stepped closer, pushing up against me.

Pushing him back and looking down, I continued before he could get a word in. "I found out who you were tied to on the internet and then you started dragging me down a dark passage after I told you why I'm here. So, what would you have me think?"

He let out a soft chuckle as he gently took me by the shoulders and pulled me closer. Placing his hand under my chin, Luder softly raised my head. "I'm sorry if I scared you." He said, looking at me with a slight smile on his lips. "I just wanted some privacy where the whole world wouldn't know what was happening. This is a big thing, you know."

I pulled my head out of his hand and looked to the side, feeling a bit guilty, thinking he was about to get rid of his problems. After the time we spent together, however short it was, I should have known.

"Let's go to the office so we can talk." He said as he started walking out before me. Luder opened the door at the end of the passage and waited for me to follow. As I passed him and scanned the room, I noticed him checking his watch.

The room was a similar size to the one in the warehouse. However, it was filled with cabinets, shelves, two tables, and a couple of chairs. On the shelves were a variety of books. What caught my eye was one in particular. The cover was old, but the name was clear.

Stepping closer, the title read *The Art of War*. This was out of place as most other books were on business management or food and related topics.

"I'm sorry, are you late for something?" I asked, turning to him while raising my eyebrows.

"It's fine," he replied, closing the door. "This is important. So, you said you are pregnant, and you are sure the baby is mine?" he asked, coming closer.

I turned and walked to the table in the middle of the room. "Yes, I only found out now," I said, stopping and leaning against the table. "You are the father; there is no man in my life currently. What do you think of me, I told you, I don't do things like that." I added, grinning.

How could he ask something like that? What kind of woman did he think I was? I felt my anger rising as I considered his words.

"Look," I said, stepping forward with my hands in my sides. "I only came here to inform you I was keeping the child. We are not a couple or anything and that is fine by me. I don't mind if you want to be part of the baby's life. It is up to you, though."

Luder stood frozen as I spoke. His eye appeared to develop a shimmer and glaze over. I felt a knot forming in my stomach, and I burned to reach out and touch his cheek. But I knew this wasn't a good idea. This life wasn't for me and surely not something I wanted for my child.

Pushing the feelings down and clearing my mind, I took a piece of paper from my pocket. "This is my number if you want to contact me," I said as I held it out for him to take.

Luder looked at the paper with a blank expression. I wondered if my handwriting was clear enough. I stepped closer and pushed it into his jacket pocket. Walking around him to the door, I glanced back.

"No strings, Luder," I said as I reached for the door handle. I felt his hand closing gently around my arm as he stepped up behind me. He pushed the door closed again and turned me to face him.

Chapter 9 - Luder

Looking down into her eyes, I understood why she was shining so brightly. I have heard people say a woman glows when she's carrying a child, but Skyler was sparkling. Her beauty was just filling the room, and my heart swelled.

"No," I stated. "This is preposterous." Once the words left my mouth, I realized they sounded very harsh. My voice rose as I spoke, and the result wasn't what I intended.

"What is?" Skyler asked softly as she tried to move backward. Her eyes were wide and filled with what I could only imagine was fear.

But I wasn't about to let her go. I walked forward as she moved back until she stood against the door. I placed my hands beside her head on both sides, pressing up against her, basically pinning her to the door.

"Family is everything," I whispered, leaning closer. "I will not have my child growing up in a broken home, hun." I could feel her breath touching my lips.

Skyler glanced from side to side at my hands. She placed hers against my chest and tried to push me back. "It's not your choice. I am the mother, and we aren't married." She spat at me. I could hear a minor quiver in her voice as she spoke.

Her hands were burning my chest where they lay, and I felt my heart rate picking up. If she only knew what she was doing to me. My blood rushed through my body, traveling southward. Soon, my mind would be invaded with other ideas. I had to stay focused, I thought, shaking my head slightly.

"Oh, but it is, and we are to be married right now. You are the mother. The mother of my child." I huffed as she forcefully pushed at my chest. She was waking the beast without even knowing it. She glanced up with a fire in her eyes.

I thought if she only knew how alluring she was at this moment while trying to calm my emotions. The fire in this woman was something new. It was the ultimate turn-on. She didn't know how she was driving me mad with lust.

"No, there is no way I am marrying you," she shot out at me as she ducked to try and get out under my arm.

I grabbed her around the waist and pulled her into my arms, holding her a bit tighter. Her demeanor changed as I tried to keep her calm. I knew this was now going to be a struggle. She might disappear if I let her go, and I couldn't have that. I had to take control of the situation without scaring her.

"Look," I said, twisting her around so she could face me. "I can provide you and our child with a good life, and I want to do it. Family is more important to me than you will ever know." I was hoping to convince her that marrying me was the only thing to do, the right thing.

"No," she said, pulling back. She had more strength than I imagined, but it could be adrenaline. "I came to you so you could have a part in the child's life. But I am not going to marry you, Luder. Now let me go."

"It really wasn't that bad, was it?" I inquired softly, looking into her eyes. "Didn't you enjoy my company," I added, smiling broadly. "And all that followed, the reason we are here now?"

Skyler turned her gaze away as a soft grin formed on her luscious lips. She remembered, and she enjoyed it too, I felt sure of this. But if she wasn't going to agree, I would have to do what was needed.

"So," I said, taking her by her shoulders and pushing her back against the door. Moving up against her, I asked again. "Let's get married, yes."

My mind was traveling a hundred miles an hour. Her juicy lips were so tempting that I just wanted to kiss her. The throbbing in my pants and the stiffening weren't ideal, but I would calm the beast in a bit.

Her smile faded quickly. "No, Luder, I told you I'm not interested. Let's just leave it at that. You can be part of the child's life, but I am not marrying you." Skyler shoved me harder this time, catching me off guard as my mind wasn't with us. "You can be glad I even came to you with this offer."

As I stepped back, she turned and opened the door. "No," I spat as I stepped up beside her and slammed the door shut. "This is not up for debate." Every muscle in my body ached as I knew there was only one way to make this happen.

Locking the door and removing the key, I took out my phone and texted Ashan to let him know he would have to go without me. I told him something had come up that I had to deal with first and would explain it all later.

Turning my attention back to Skyler, I noticed she had not moved. She stood facing the door with her hands up against it. "Skyler," I said, placing a hand on her shoulder.

"I'm sorry, it didn't have to be this way, but you aren't giving me any other option." I pulled a chair up to her side. "Have a seat, hun. I need to make a couple of calls." She glanced at me over her shoulder, her eyes were filled with anger. But she took the chair and sat down, still facing the door.

"I'm not staying, no matter what you say or do," she said angrily.

I walked to the desk and called Roman. Whispering, I explained briefly why I couldn't go with Ashan. I told him I was going to my place and would catch up with them once everything was taken care of.

Placing the phone down, I considered my options. I could drag her out screaming and kicking. No, I could subdue her and carry her out. Shaking my head, I knew that wouldn't work as I had nothing here to subdue her with.

Frustrated, I looked through the drawers. There was nothing here.

CHAPTER 10 - SKYLER

I couldn't hear what he was saying to the person on the phone, but I felt scared. He locked the door and took the key; he was insistent on marrying me. This is not what I expected, but then, on the other hand, what did I think was going to happen?

After all, he was part of Bratva. I felt fear mixing with my anger as I scanned the room. I had to find a way to get out; why didn't I tell Mathieu I was coming here? Well, if I had told him that, I would have had to tell him why, and I wasn't ready for his criticism.

My life was a mess; I felt my heart beating quickly. The situation wasn't ideal, but I knew I would find a solution somewhere along the line. He let me go the first time, maybe he would again.

As he placed the phone back on its perch, I felt a shiver run up my spine as fear took over. The window was too small to get out of, I would have to wait until we were outside. I told myself I had to formulate a plan as I heard him walking toward me. I took a deep breath, trying to calm my nerves.

Luder came around and stood before me, grinning. "Come on, we have to get going," he said, holding out his hand.

"No," I replied, trying to keep the quiver out of my voice. The tears burned behind my eyes, but I fought to keep them from showing. I jumped up out of the chair and moved to the back of it. Holding the chair between us, I wasn't sure what I intended to do, but I didn't want to go with him.

Luder grabbed the chair and shoved it to the side, almost pulling my arms out of their sockets. He stepped up to me and gripped my arm tightly as I fell forward. Pulling me up against him and to the door. He unlocked it before glancing at me. "You don't have to make this harder than it needs to be, you know." He said as we headed down the passage.

Entering the bar area, I noticed the place was deserted. There were no staff, barman, cleaners, or anyone present. I felt my heart sinking as I realized there was no one to see me being dragged against my will, being abducted.

Outside, he pulled me around the side of the building. There were a couple of cars and guards standing around. We stopped next to one of the cars, and Luder nodded at the driver. The dark-haired man opened the back door for us.

"You know screaming won't help. They all work for us," Luder said as he started to shove me inside.

I looked around frantically; there was no way out. My tears couldn't be kept back anymore, and they rolled down my cheeks as he got in beside me. I moved away and tried the other side door. It was locked and wouldn't open, I was trapped. Sitting up against the door, I allowed my tears to run freely as I stared out the window.

We drove down towards the ocean, but I didn't recognize the roads we took. The area was unfamiliar to me. I felt my stomach turning as I wondered what he was going to do with me. If family was so important to him, I was sure he wouldn't kill me, but what would he do? I glanced at him, trying to assess the danger I might be in.

Luder sat there calmly as a moonlit lake. I wondered how he kept his cool when I felt like my world was coming to an end. It must be because he was used to doing things like this. With his family ties and all, I assured myself that there would be others somewhere.

"Don't look so upset, hun," he said out of the blue. "It was fun. Didn't you like it, did I misread you?"

Stunned at his words, I swallowed the lump growing in my throat. "This is not why I came to you, even if I enjoyed it," I replied softly, trying to regain my composure.

Turning to me, he continued. "You have to admit, the first time was something, wasn't it?" His smile brightened his face, and I looked back out the window as my heart skipped a beat. This wasn't a time to have such feelings, no matter how attracted to him I was.

This was not what I wanted, I assured myself. Did he really think I wanted to be kidnapped, he was insane.

"Just admit it, and this journey will be so much easier for you," he continued. "The rush, the adrenaline of being captured, leads to great sex, don't you think?"

I could hear the excitement in his voice as he spoke and felt my body wanting him. But I kept my mind focused as this wasn't what I wanted, even if my body wanted him. I was confused at the need and anger tumbling through me as one.

"No," I replied sully without even looking at him.

The car slowed, entered a large gate, and came to a stop on the shore. There was a no-trespassing sign huge as life, and it looked like we were at a private dock. Luder got out and walked around to my side. He opened the door and held out his hand.

"Come, Skyler," he said. "Don't make it hard."

I shifted out of the car, ignoring his gesture, and looked around. To the back was the big gate with fencing running in both directions as far as I could see. There were also guards every two or three meters apart along the fence. Before us was the dock with about five boats at the sides.

Luder reached out and took my hand. I glanced up at him as I pulled my hand back. "No, take me home." I spat at him as I stepped back to get into the car.

Once again, he grabbed my arm and started pulling me towards the boats. "No, help me, please," I screamed, pulling back. I wasn't going to go in one of those; this was it. I had to get out, or I wouldn't ever see my life again.

Luder pulled me close and picked me up. He threw me over his shoulder as if I weighed nothing. He held my legs against his chest as I tried kicking. I formed my hands into fists and laid them down on his back. But nothing seemed to faze him as he kept moving.

The guards weren't faded by my screaming either; they just kept doing what they were. I wasn't sure which boat we got onto as he pulled me back over his shoulder into his arms, stepping on board one of the yachts. I tried to wiggle out of his arms, but his grip was powerful. He carried me down into the yacht, down a short hallway, and into a room.

Stepping in, he kicked the door closed behind us before dropping me onto a soft bed. I scurried away from him, sitting up against the window. Looking over my shoulder, I noticed the bars across the window. Glancing around, I noticed the other two windows also had bars.

This wasn't a room, it was a jail, I thought as I noticed the locks on the door. It was a large room. There was a big old wooden table towards one side, and a small kitchen set-up with a fridge, kettle, etc. On the other side, then there were also some cupboards, shelves with books and cabinets.

I had to admit the bed was quite comfortable and soft. Luder walked to the fridge and poured a glass of fresh juice. As he handed it to me, I wondered if he had been keeping tabs on me. Or was it only a coincidence that he knew I liked fruit juice?

"Right then," he said, sitting on the end of the bed.

I pulled my legs up to my chest to create some space between us. Sipping at the juice, I glared at him across the rim of the glass. My crying had stopped, and my fear was slightly subdued, but I wasn't ready to be entertained by him. The juice, however, was welcome as my throat was parched.

"Give me your phone, Skyler," he ordered.

I lowered the glass and looked him in the eye. "No, it's my phone, you can't have it." I placed the glass down and moved my purse behind me. My phone was in my suit pocket, but he didn't know that. Maybe I could fool him and tell him I left it at home if he didn't find it in my purse.

Luder moved closer and started to pull me down on the bed. He took hold of the purse strap and pulled as I slid down. I was clutching it for dear life, but he got it out of my grip after a while. By the time he managed to pull it from me, we were lying sideways on the bed.

Jumping up, Luder looked like a small child who had won a prize. I couldn't help but smile as he jumped up and down. He wasn't acting as I would have expected, and I wondered if Bratva was as bad as people made it out to be. He wasn't using a gun on me or frightening me in any way except for kidnapping me.

He searched through my purse but couldn't find my phone. After a bit, he looked at me. "Where is it?" he asked. His voice had a serious tone, and all the ease I felt dissipated.

"Isn't it in there?" I replied, raising my eyebrows. "Maybe I forgot to take it this morning," I added, shaking my head. "I was in a rush, so it may still be at home."

Luder looked at my purse and then at me with curiosity showing on his face. "You like to play games, don't you?" he asked as he dropped my purse to the floor and stepped closer to the bed.

"No," I replied, trying to sound confident. "It must be at home, I swear."

Luder didn't look convinced. I moved back up and got off the other side of the bed as he leaned forward, reaching out for me. "It's at home," I said, walking backward.

He jumped onto the bed and lunged at me. "I don't have time for this now, Skyler." He snapped as he grabbed me by the shoulders. I turned and tried to push my hands up between his, hoping to get out of his grip. But it didn't do anything except maybe upset him.

"Stop playing games," Luder exclaimed as he turned me and shoved me back onto the bed. He sat over me on the bed as he patted me down.

"Get off me," I screamed, trying to take hold of his hands.

Luder pulled my hands together above my head and pinned them with one hand. "Stop," he said harshly as his other hand trailed down my sides.

I felt my stomach turning as he softly left a tingling sensation down my body. He felt my pant pockets and discovered what he was seeking. Forcing his large hand into the pocket made the material tear as he extracted my phone.

"Don't ever lie to me again," he said as he got up and shook the phone in the air.

"Luder, please, I'm sorry," I tried reasoning with him.

He walked to the door, pushing the phone into his pocket before turning and looking back at me. "No," he said. "I'll be back, you can wait here. There is juice, water, and food if you feel the need."

"What if I need the bathroom," I tried, hoping he would leave the door unlocked. "I won't leave, I promise."

"I have seen what you want, but there will be time for it when I return." He said, opening the door. "There's a bucket under the table if your need is too big." He added smirking.

"What?" I spat at him as I rose from the bed. "This is inhumane, you can't keep me locked up here."

Chapter 11 - Luder

"Inhumane?" I retorted as I slammed the door closed again. "You have no idea what inhumane is, hun."

"I want to go home," she screamed.

"Well, that's not going to happen," I replied calmly.

"Give me my phone back," she added, storming at me with her fists up. I stood as she beat her fists into my chest.

Grabbing her wrists, I shoved her gently back. "This isn't going to work," I said, smiling.

Stepping across the floor quickly, Skyler moved back to the window between the bed and the cupboard. She looked like a rat running from a trap, then turned and banged her tiny fists against the bullet-proof window as she started screaming louder.

For some reason, this made my desire for her intensify. I felt my veins filling with fire as I walked closer. She was a wild one and made my senses light up.

I grabbed her around the waist and placed one hand over her mouth as I walked up behind her. "Enough," I whispered in her ear as I pushed her up against the window. There was a heat between us I couldn't explain. "It's not going to help you any; no one will hear you."

Letting go of her mouth, I held her hips. "Would you rather have some fun?" I added, nibbling her earlobe. Skyler twisted slightly sideways in my arms.

My hand slipped to the crotch of her pants, gripping her pussy firmly but soft. She had stopped screaming and was now gasping for air.

I felt her calm down in my grip. Pulling her with me toward the bed, I continued to whisper to her. "I can be very accommodating if you stop fighting me, Skyler.," I added, feeling the beast within fully awake.

My hands moved to her middle as I undid the buttons of her pants. She placed her hands over mine and softly tried to pull them away. But her resistance was weak, and I knew she wanted me just as much as I burned for her in that moment. There was too much tension in the air. It had to go somewhere.

I shoved my hand into her pants and found my way back to her pussy. My other hand moved up to her breasts. She arched into me as I moved. I grabbed her suit jacket between her breasts and yanked it open. Buttons went flying as the two parts came loose.

I pushed my finger up her vagina as I ripped her top open, exposing her delicious breasts. Skyler bent slightly forward as she gasped at the air around us. Her hands moved to my sides and dug into my thighs as my fingers moved in and out.

Pulling my hand out of her pants, I ripped off her bra before turning her to me. Her eyes were sparkling as I leaned in and kissed her. She fumbled at the buttons of my shirt as I pushed her pants and panties down her thighs.

My dick was throbbing wildly in my pants, and I had to get them off. I shoved her back on the bed naked as the day she was born. Her beautiful curves made my mind numb as she smiled up at me, licking her lips. There was no time to take my clothes off. I ripped my shirt open and, with lightning speed, lowered my pants. Skyler sat up on the bed and pulled me closer.

She wrapped her fingers around my cock, and I felt myself floating as she gently pushed back and pulled forward. Her free hand moved around, grabbing my ass. She leaned forward and placed the tip of my cock in her mouth. I inhaled strongly as I looked down.

My hands wrapped around her head as I drove my fingers through her hair and pulled her head in. She moved her other hand also back to hold my ass. My body shook with delight as she sucked my dick. I directed her head as I forced it forward and pulled back in continuous movements. She moaned ever so delightfully as her lips loosened and tightened.

Soon, I felt my muscles spasm as I came into her mouth. I roared with delight as she slowly pulled back. Finding my composure, I bent forward and picked her up into my arms. She gave me a strength I never knew I had. I could live with this, I thought as I walked to the table.

I wiped the items from the top and placed her on the table. Lowering her to the table, I left a trail of kisses down her neck. My mouth sought out her nipples. She grabbed the sides of the table as I softly bit down and pulled first one nipple up and then the other. As I played with her breasts, she shifted lightly from one side to the other.

She enveloped her legs around my waist as her breathing became irregular. We were good together, I thought as I pushed my fingers into her pussy. She lifted her butt, pushing her body up to me as my fingers moved in and out. She moaned with pleasure.

Feeling her body against mine made my heart beat a little faster. There were sparks between us. I grabbed her legs and pulled them loose. Moving my hands up her thighs, I took hold of her hips, pinning her to the table. I placed kisses down her stomach as I moved down, kneeling between her legs.

Her pussy was radiating with heat and moisture as I licked her. Skyler tried to shift as I found her clitoris with my tongue, but I held her tight. She wrapped her legs around my head as I slowly moved up and down her vagina. Her breathing was now coming out in shudders. I glanced up at her and smiled as she grabbed hold of my head.

She couldn't resist me, she wanted more, and I had no issue pleasing her. I softly bit her clitoris and pulled at it. Skyler pushed my head into her as she lifted her body from the table. I moved my tongue up and down her pussy a couple of times quickly before penetrating her with it.

Skyler let out a cry of excitement as my tongue played inside her. Her grip on my hair increased as I pushed my tongue in and out. Soon, she was screaming as she came. Her body shook in my hands. I stood and penetrated her with my throbbing dick.

Grabbing her legs, I pulled her closer and shoved hard into her. Skyler moved her head from side to side with her eyes closed as she moaned. I pulled her up into my arms and lifted her from the table.

I walked over to the door and pinned her up against it as I felt my dick craving more. She exhaled deeply as I penetrated her even deeper. I felt my legs shaking as I moved her up and down on my shaft.

We came together in a shuddering of gasps. I felt her nails digging into my back as I softly lowered her to the floor. For a moment, I stood holding her to my body as our breathing started to regulate. I hugged her tightly before picking her up again and placing her down on the bed. Without a word, I turned to the cupboard, grabbed my clothing, and got dressed.

Turning to face her, I noticed she had pulled the sheet up over her. I walked over and placed a tender kiss on her cheek. "I'll be back shortly," I breathed out as I moved to the door. "Next to the bookshelf is a passage to the bathroom," I added.

Walking out and locking the door behind me, I felt amazing. Her touch still surged through me, giving me renewed strength. I had never felt so at ease, so filled with power as I was at that moment. I felt invincible, and it was a feeling I could get used to.

I was walking on clouds as I left the yacht. I gave the two guards on the dock instructions to stay close and make sure she didn't get out or anyone in. Once they were in place, I headed to town to join the family. I called Roman to let him know she was locked up tight and I was heading to Ashan.

"Good," Roman replied. "We are all in place and ready to go."

I arrived at the warehouse minutes after Ashan and some of the guards had entered. Following the path we had discussed, I entered from a side panel that had been cut open. As I moved around some crates and barrels, I heard Ashan mumbling something, and I froze.

"No, this can't be," I whispered as I came around a crate and saw the two guards down on the floor. One was still alive, it seemed he had only been shot twice. Once in the leg and once in the chest, I noticed as I knelt next to him. The other one was dead. It looked like he had taken the majority of bullets. His chest was covered in holes, and a pool of blood surrounded him.

The guard beside me tugged my jacket and pointed to the back of the building. I rose, furious. Why did he not wait for me? If Ashan wasn't dead, I was going to kill him myself. I headed down between the crates to the back. There were a lot less of Anchony's men than I expected.

Seeing an opportunity as most had gone back out to check the perimeter, I snuck up on the one closest to me. He had his back turned as I stepped out of the shadows of the crates. Taking his head in my hands, I snapped his neck. Ashan looked up at me and smiled. Pulling my gun, I hurried over to him and undid the ropes around his hands.

As he stood up from the chair, his face all bloody and his one eye seemingly swollen shut, he shot past me. Turning, I saw the men streaming in through the wide-open double doors. We took out the five guards storming at us and then set the charges.

Exiting the building, we met with some of the Anchony family. Bullets went flying in both directions as they tried to enter the warehouse. We had to keep them out for another two minutes as the plan was to detonate at precisely five.

Moving from the door of the building to the steel container a couple of meters forward, we lay down bullets. Stopping behind the container, I saw Ashan had been hit. Blood was running down his left shoulder.

"Brother," I exclaimed, pulling my tie loose from my neck and pressing it to his shoulder. "You've been hit."

Ashan looked down and smiled at me. "It's fine, just a scratch." He said but I could see his face draining of blood.

I waved to our guards waiting at the gate, showing them to come closer. Another session of bullets went flying around us as they came over. Two took Ashan as the other two made a human shield, running back to the cars with him.

Stepping out from behind the container, I rained down on the enemy before retreating back to the safety of the large steel container. Checking my watch, I saw it was time. I stepped out again and shot some unsuspecting Anchony men as they were coming closer. I ducked a couple of bullets and ran for the cars. Jumping in through the open door, I felt something nick my calve.

But there was no time to worry about it. I pulled the door closed as we sped off. Turning in my seat, I saw the explosion taking place. A large cloud of fire and smoke filled the air as the charges went off one after another.

As we drove back to the club, we could see clouds filling the air throughout the city. Today, we took care of business, I thought as I pulled my pants leg up to have a look at the burning sensation on my leg. Just a scratch, the bullet only nicked my skin as it passed. Back at the club, Ivan had the doctor check on Ashan as we all gave an account of our actions.

It was about seven when we broke up and could return home. Ashan was fine and would spend the night at Roman's so Karine could keep an eye on the wound. However, the doctor was able to remove the bullet, and no permanent damage could be seen. I wished them all a good night and felt relieved that Ashan would be good.

As I drove back, I couldn't help but ponder on the extraordinary strength I felt during the afternoon. The power that Skyler filled me with. I had to keep her close. We may not be each other's type or first choice. But, except for our baby, she also gave me something else.

I couldn't explain it, but she made me better.

Chapter 12 - Skyler

I watched in silence as he got dressed and left. The sex was good between us, but was it enough? I lay for a while, allowing my body to soak in the feelings still rushing through me. He had a way with me, I didn't know why, but I wanted his touch. My mind and body fought as each wanted something else.

My mind kept telling me to get out as soon as possible while my body craved his touch. My heart was a mess as I didn't know what I wanted.

After a while, I sat up, remembering Bunny was home alone, and fear started creeping in. I scanned the room again, wondering if there was a way out. Who would feed Bunny if I didn't return home? Maybe Mathieu would come around looking for me. No, I thought as I got up. He was always so busy, but he did call me occasionally. Maybe he would, and once he saw I was missing, he would call the cops.

Gathering my clothes, I looked in the drawers for a knife or something sharp I could try on the door locks. There was food and a variety of drinks in the fridge, but all the cutlery was plastic. Right, I thought as I broke a plastic knife in two; why would he have anything I could use to escape here?

Walking up to one of the windows, I considered the strength of the bars. They seemed quite solid as I pulled and tried shaking them. I rummaged through the items Luder had pushed to the floor when he placed me down on the table and smiled, remembering his touch.

The floor was scattered with papers, pens, and a paperweight. I picked up the paperweight and felt its heaviness. "This might work," I said as I turned and headed back to the window.

I tried hitting the window with the paperweight, but it didn't even scratch it. "What the hell," I screamed. What was the window made of? I took a couple of steps back and threw it at the window. The paperweight bounced against the glass and came back quickly, almost hitting me. I had to duck as it came whirling back.

I heard it smashing into something in the kitchen. My veins filled with ice as I slowly turned. I couldn't see where it landed at that moment, which was probably not good. I fell to the ground as tears pushed up and a lump formed in my throat. "No," I screamed as I felt fear creeping back in. I convinced myself there had to be a way out as I stood back up.

I found a baseball bat while digging through the cupboards, shelves, and cabinets. I swung at the door, windows, and walls and even tried the roof. After a while, my arms burnt and felt heavy from all the exercise. I dropped the bat to the floor, looking at the couple of dents I made.

Nothing, not even one crack. What was this place? I sank to my knees placing my head into my hands, and sobbed. I wasn't going to get out ever. In the end, I would have to go along with whatever Luder wanted I thought as I crawled up onto the bed.

Hugging the soft pillow, I cried unstoppably for quite some time. This was the end of my life. I would never see Bunny or my brother again. My heart felt as if it was going to explode as my chest struggled to find air.

This place was off the normal routes and hidden. Not even the cops would find me. After a while, my tears started drying up. My breathing regulated as I felt fatigue set in. I wanted to sleep, my body and mind were tired of fighting. But I didn't dare close my eyes.

No, I thought as I sat up. I needed to devise a plan. I had to get out of here. He would be back later, he said. I got up and collected the bat from the middle of the floor where I had dropped it.

Yes, I thought as I walked back to the bed. When he comes back, I'll wait on the side of the door. If I swing hard enough, I could probably knock him out. I drank the rest of the juice, which was now hot, before pouring myself another glass.

I collected the chair from behind the desk and sat on it next to the door, waiting. The day passed slowly, and I decided to take a short nap. Waking after some time, I noticed the sun started setting as the room darkened. Next to the door were two switches. I toggled the first one, but nothing happened.

The second one lit up the room in a soft yellowish glow. Really, I thought as I stood and went to the fridge. He couldn't even put in a decent light. I was feeling weak and puckish as I searched through the contents of the fridge for something to eat.

It held a couple of glass jars; some I assumed were jellies, others contained pickles. There was an apple and banana, but I wasn't sure, even though they still appeared fine. On the lower shelf were a couple of plastic bowls with who knew what in them. I grabbed a bottle of pickles and a plastic fork before returning to the chair at the door.

I was sure he would be returning soon, and I wanted to be ready. About halfway through the bottle of pickles, I felt my stomach turning. Closing the bottle, I held it out before me. "This wasn't such a good idea," I said. I got up and placed the bottle back in the fridge.

My stomach was now aching. It was a dull pain, but it was there. I considered that even though it was bottled, I didn't know how old it was. I might have just caught something, and I didn't know how long Luder was still going to be.

Sitting back down on the chair, I pulled my legs onto it and hugged them. A slow and steady throbbing started at the back of my head. No, no, no, I thought as my mind started running with ideas of what I could have caught.

Never take something from strangers, my mother always used to say. But, in my own defense, he's not quite a stranger. Plus, he said I should have something. But how was I to know it wasn't poisoned?

Watching the sun setting outside, I wondered if Luder would do something like that. I felt sure he wouldn't, it could just be that I consumed too much sour. I did feel a bit nauseated as well.

He would be back soon, and then I could go, I told myself as I dropped the bat to the floor. How could I even consider hitting him with it if I could barely move?

Sliding off the chair, I slowly walked back to bed. I lay holding the pillow to my stomach, curled into a small bundle. My head ached almost as much as my stomach. I didn't know where I should be holding. I closed my eyes and tried to focus on something else.

My mind kept going to Bunny all alone at home, and I didn't want to think about it. I filled his food and water before I left, but he has never been alone all day and night. I felt tears threatening to worsen my mood as I lifted my head in an attempt to stiffen the tears.

There was a noise outside and I looked out the window, hoping to see a light or something. I didn't know what I was hoping for, but there was nothing. Then I heard footsteps, and I knew he had returned.

Although I didn't want to be here, I felt a slight flash of happiness hearing him return. It could be due to me feeling sick or that I was feeling something because of the child. At this time, I couldn't be sure. I just knew I was glad he was back.

Chapter 13 - Luder

I parked my car close to the docks and sat for a bit, watching the guards move around. The area was quiet as usual, with nothing much happening. Getting out of my car, two of the guards walked closer.

"Evening sir," they said in unison.

"Evening, any developments?" I inquired as I headed towards the docks.

The two guards followed closely behind me as I moved. "Nothing to report." They add.

Stepping onto the docks, I turn and face them. "Good, thanks, that will be all," I said as I showed them to continue their rounds.

"There was, however," one of the men started saying and then looked at the other.

"Come on, spit it out, there was what?" I asked rushed.

"Well, you see, we were walking the docks and heard an awful banging noise coming from your yacht, sir." The other one added.

"Okay, thanks," I said, feeling my insides turning. What had Skyler been up to?

They turned and walked off. I walked along the dock slowly, listening to the night sounds of bugs and the water softly lapping at the bottom of the yachts. I loved being out here, it had a calming effect on me.

Stepping onto the deck of my yacht, I told the two guards stationed there to return to their normal positions. I headed down to the lower level picking up Skyler's phone as I went. She had three missed calls from a guy named Mathieu.

I recognized the name. It was the guy who was with Domique the day I met Skyler. Maybe that was why she looked so worried when I shot him. I concluded that she must be part of them as I headed to the room. I felt my anger rise as I unlocked the door and stepped inside. She was lying down on the bed, but the place was a mess. Scanning the room, I realized she was looking for something while I was gone.

There were scratches on the windows and dents in the furniture. In the kitchen, the shelf with the pots seemed to have broken. Next to the chair behind the door lay my bat. I considered that she may have wanted to hit me with it at some point.

"Looks like you had fun," I said closing the door and listening for the automatic locking. Turning to her, I drop the phone on the foot of the bed. "You have a guy calling you. Three times today I see."

I pulled the chair standing by the door closer and sat down. Taking a deep breath I continue. "How must I trust you when you say the baby is mine? If there is a baby? When you can't be honest with me."

Skyler slowly lifted her head and looked at me. She seemed a bit pale. "Have you eaten?" I asked as I stood up and walked to the small kitchen. "I'll make us some supper; you must be starving."

"I ate," Skyler replied softly behind me. "I feel sick, I think the pickles are off."

I glanced at her over my shoulder and grinned. "No, it may be nerves causing you to feel ill. But, then again, if you are pregnant, having only pickles to eat might not have been such a good idea."

I poured her a glass of water and walked back to the bed. "Here," I said. "Sit up and drink it. Then tell me about this guy who keeps on calling you."

Skyler slowly sat up and took the glass from me. After a couple of sips, she placed the glass down and pulled her phone closer, looking at the screen. Smiling, she glanced up at me.

"Who is he?" I asked as I took the phone back and stared at the screen. "Is he the real father? Are you playing me?"

"Oh my," Skyler uttered as she fell back to the bed. "No, Mathieu is my brother." She admitted, laughing lightly. "He works for a broker firm around the corner, he's a consultant." Skyler stopped laughing and held her stomach again.

"Can you tell me more about your brother?" I inquired.

"Well," she said, wiping at the corners of her mouth. "He's sixteen years older, and as we grew up without a father, he has always looked out for me. You can say he was the father I never had in a sense."

I nodded. "And you said he is a broker?" I prodded.

"He has a degree, but he consults. He only advises on best business practices. How to invest and where. Why do you need a broker consultant?" she asked, picking up the water and drinking the last bit.

Grinning at her, I shook my head, "No, thanks. I was just wondering."

"Really," she said, moving closer. "I can call him, and you can have a chat."

I felt her phone vibrating in my pocket. Standing, I took it out and looked at the screen. As if, somehow, Mathieu knew we were talking about him, his name showed on the caller ID.

"I would have to answer him at some stage, or he will know something is wrong," Skyler spoke as she rose and walked closer.

Killing the call, I pushed the phone back into my pocket. "We will see," I said as I walked around the table and pulled a bottle of vodka from the drawer. "First, I think we should talk," I added, glancing at her.

Skyler stood on the other side of the table. I couldn't quite figure out what she was up to, but I was sure she was working an angel. She placed her hands on the end of the table and leaned forward.

"Sure, what do you want to talk about," she said, smiling.

I walked back to the bed and sat down on the chair. I felt her watching me as I moved. I patted the end of the bed.

"Come, sit with me," I said, glancing over my shoulder.

Skyler came strolling over, slowly watching me. She sat down and folded her hands in her lap.

"What I'm about to tell you may sound a bit, well," I said, pulling the chair closer and taking her hands in mine. "It may sound unbelievable." I finished watching her reaction.

"I think we are past the unlikely stage, don't you think," she said as she pulled her hand from mine and waved it around. "This was already farfetched, I mean, who would have thought you would kidnap me, twice."

"Okay, I get it," I replied, standing up and moving to the small kitchen.

Looking back at her, Skyler was perched up on her elbows, lying on her stomach on the bed, smiling at me. "So, how about I make supper while we talk?"

CHAPTER 14 - SKYLER

"Sure, if you think you can give me something that won't make me feel worse," I said while shifting my position on the bed.

"I'm not the one who made you sick," he responded calmly, turning to the table. "You know your brother can't be trusted."

"What," I spat at him, rising from the bed and walking over to the table. "You know nothing about him. How can you make such accusations?" I asked as I slammed my hands down on the desk.

"Calm down," Luder said as he moved and opened the fridge again to check its contents. "I can tell you more, but you have to calm down first." He added.

"No," I hissed as I walked up and down the small room. "You have nothing to say as you know nothing, so just stay quiet and make the food."

He glanced at me over his shoulder. I had stopped and looked at the books on the shelf by the door. My mind was whirling with his words. I knew my brother, he didn't, he had no right to say that. Keeping me locked up here wasn't helping my anger either, as I felt the blood in my veins boiling. Glancing at the door, I remembered I hadn't seen him lock it when he came in.

Looking back at him, I noticed him grabbing some meat from the freezer compartment and placing it in a pan on the small stove. I thought this might be my only opportunity.

He had just lit the gas and placed the meat in the pan. I moved slowly and quietly to the door. Turning the knob, I felt it was locked.

Back at the table, he had just chucked his jacket over the side of the other chair. Moving back slowly, I leaned over the chair, pretending to be feeling ill.

Feeling through his pockets, I found the key. He was still busy with the meat, so I moved quickly. Unlocking and opening the door, I sprinted out and ran onto the dock. I knew he would be coming after me, but I had to try. I wasn't going to stay. I couldn't allow him to keep me here and then he dared to insult my brother as well.

"Skyler," I heard him calling out after me. I was already on the dock heading for the gate. "Skyler, stop," he called again. "There's nowhere to go, hun."

Glancing over my shoulder, I saw him on the dock. I had to run faster, I thought as I turned my attention back to the gate. Sure, it was locked, but maybe I could climb over it.

I felt my lungs burning as I reached the gate and started pulling myself up. My legs were tired, but I had to get out. I was about halfway up the gate when I felt two hands grabbing my ankles and pulling me down. I held onto the gate as long as possible, trying to kick while screaming.

My grip slipped as my hands became sweaty, and I plunged to the ground. Luckily, I didn't hit the ground as the two guards pulling me caught me. They came out of nowhere, I felt sure they had heard Luder calling. If not for that, I might have made it.

I had no idea where I would have gone if I got over the gate. But I would have had a chance. I would have had a chance if I had just run into the bushes.

The two guards that had grabbed me held me upright as Luder came to a stop before us. I was still struggling and screaming in their arms as he straightened himself out. Luder grabbed me around the waist and thanked the guards before turning and heading back to the yacht.

"You know there is no one to hear you. Please stop screaming," he said a bit out of breath and clearly irritated.

"You let me go, you have no right, let me go," I spat as he dragged me along.

He pulled me back onto the yacht and down to the cabin. He locked the door and placed the key in his pant pocket before letting go of me.

69

"Now then, did you enjoy your little run?" he asked. "You're not sick if you can still sprint like that," he added.

I suddenly realized the smell of burnt meat had filled the room, and so did he. "Look at what you made me do now," he said as he stepped up to the stove and turned it off. "Now, neither of us has any supper."

Crossing my arms over my chest, I pushed my lips out into a pout as I walked to the window, staring out. "I don't care," I answered, hearing him making a call.

He called one of his men outside to get some Chinese take-out. While we waited, he trashed the burnt meat and cleaned the stove. Once he was satisfied with the kitchen, he started collecting all the papers he had thrown off the desk earlier. "Where's my paperweight," he asked.

I strolled over, quietly, and slowly. He didn't look up as I came to stand beside him. Was he angry at me, I wondered. He had no right to be upset, I was being held against my will. But, if I intended on getting out, I would have to play along.

"I'm sorry," I said softly as I knelt beside him and gathered some papers. "I'm not sure where the paperweight went, though."

"No," he replied dryly. "It's no problem. You do you, and I'll do me, okay." He took the papers from my hands and stood up.

I felt his eyes on me as I walked back to the bed and sat down on the edge. After a while, there was a knock at the door, and I knew it had to be our food. Luder placed the papers on the table and walked over to the door. He unlocked it and collected the bags from the big man outside.

"Here," he said, holding out the bags toward me.

I took the two bags and peeked inside as he locked the door again, I was not going to get out of there anytime soon, I thought as I glanced at him. For now, my fight is over. I felt my stomach grumbling as hunger made its presence known.

He had taken out plates while cleaning and held out a plate for me as I looked through the four meals he had ordered.

"No thanks," I said, taking a box and a packet of chopsticks. "I can eat out of the box."

He returned the plates to the cupboard and studied me for a while from across the room. I didn't look up; I still felt angry at him because he was angry at me.

Luder came over and pulled up the chair to the side of the bed before sitting down. "Skyler," he said as he picked up the Kung Pao Chicken. I glanced up as I carefully placed a dumpling in my mouth, pulling up my eyebrows.

I wasn't ready to talk, but he could talk if he wanted. "Look, there are things you don't understand." He said, opening his kung pao chicken.

He popped a chicken piece into his mouth and chewed. Once he had swallowed, he continued. "However, I now see you are not ready for the truth, which is fine."

"The truth," I spat. "You don't know anything about me or my brother. Just let me go and I'll never bother you again."

Luder stared at me as he narrowed his eyebrows. "You know that's not going to happen," he said calmly before taking another bite of his food. "If you want the truth, well, I can give it to you."

Turning on the bed with my back to him, I finished my dumplings in silence. I wondered if Mathieu would make sure Bunny had enough food and water. I felt tears forming behind my eyelids just thinking of Bunny. He would be waiting at the door for me. Somehow, I had to convince Luder to let me go, but how?

I placed the takeaway container on the bed and covered my face with my hands, rubbing at my eyes to stop the tears. I heard Luder taking away the unopened meals. Glancing sideways, I saw he had also taken the empty containers and was pouring himself a glass of vodka.

Laying on the bed, I wished I had never found him or told him about the baby. I hadn't even told Mathieu yet and now I might never get the chance. I pulled my legs up to my chest and lay in a fetal position, feeling my eyes getting heavier.

At least the nausea was gone, and I felt better. Maybe if I slept, tomorrow would be a better day. I heard Luder coming over and closed my eyes. "Your brother works for the enemy, Bratva," he said softly.

I dared not move. I wanted him to leave. He was lying, it was all a trick. He stood for a while before leaving and locking me in. He must have thought I was sleeping, but that was fine. I wanted to be alone. I thought about what he said for a long time until I finally fell asleep.

Sometime during the night, I woke as Luder returned. I heard him entering and scolding at something he kicked while trying to find his way in the dark. Smiling, I found this amusing, it was his place, and he didn't know his way around.

I felt him lying down and pulling me into his arms. I just lay silently. I didn't want any more talks with him. After a while, I heard him snoring lightly and knew he was asleep. Closing my eyes, I found sleep came quickly this time.

"Skyler, Skyler," I heard Luder calling my name, but he sounded far away.

Rubbing my eyes, I sat up. The room was still dark. For a moment, I thought I had dreamed it. Turning, I noticed he was no longer next to me on the bed. I scanned the room as my eyes adjusted to the dark.

But I was alone. I must have dreamt it. Feeling my throat scratching, I got up and walked to the fridge. I studied the room after pouring a glass of juice and drinking half in one swallow. Yes, I was alone and didn't know when he had left.

I walked to the door and put the light on. I had to find a way out, I thought as I surveyed the room. The bathroom had a tiny round window, and these large ones were made of something that didn't appear to be breakable.

Walking to the closet, I searched through its contents, but it only held his clothes. The shelves and other cabinets didn't provide anything useful either. I flopped down on the bed as my tears started flowing again. I haven't cried this much in as long as I can remember.

My heart felt heavy. I wondered where he had gone and how long he would stay. Feeling like an old rag, I decided to take a shower, but I had no clothes. "Well, then," I spoke to the closet as I opened it again. "I'll just have to wear some of his."

After a quick shower, I entered the kitchen and heated some of the leftover food as I was starving again. This was going to take some time getting used to. Having my tea at the table, I consider my options of things to do locked up in this cabin.

Strolling through the room, I somehow ended up in front of his closet. Standing there staring at his suits, my mind took a wild turn. Deciding his outfits needed some color, I experimented a little.

Grabbing a book from the shelf, I decided to do some reading while I waited for him to return.

Soon, the sun made its way through the dark and lit up the world outside. As time passed, I got bored. I decided that if he wanted to keep me here, I would make it as unpleasant as I could. Maybe he would let me go if he saw what a menace I was.

CHAPTER 15 - LUDER

Pulling into the secure parking area of Ivan's club, I wondered what had come up. It was still dark when he called and told me to attend the club. He had not given a reason, but I could hear in his voice he was upset.

I had left Skyler sleeping as she needed rest, and I hoped to return before she woke. I might even grab some breakfast on my way back. Stepping out of the car, the cool morning breeze was the first to greet me. It seemed cooler up here than down at our private docks, which was a bit weird.

Yet, the docks were surrounded by trees and shrubs, so, I guess it kept out some of the cold air even though it was by the water. I hurried to the side door and entered the club. Walking down the passage, I heard voices coming from the club area and not the office.

This too, was out of place like the early morning call. I took out my Glock as I walked into the club, unsure of what to expect. There in the middle of the room, sat Mathieu tied to a chair. On one side was Ivan and on the other side stood Roman, but other than that, the place was empty.

Holstering my gun, I walked over to them. "What is this?" I asked as I came to stand between them.

"Glad you could join us, Luder," Ivan said, tapping me on the shoulder. "We caught him breaking in here."

"What?" I responded in a raised voice. Skyler surely didn't know her brother if he was this cocky.

"The thing is," Roman said as he turned me towards him. "He says he is only looking for his sister. He said he didn't want trouble. Can you believe that?"

I looked at Mathieu while I replied. "If that was the case, he would have come during club hours and asked us instead of breaking in."

"My thought exactly," Roman replied, stepping closer to Mathieu. "I think he was planning to take something or destroy something."

"Wait, guys," Mathieu said, looking at me. "You're Luder?" he asked, scanning me up and down.

Joining Roman before him, I placed my hands on my knees and bent forward, replying with a nod.

"I went to her house as I couldn't get hold of her yesterday," he started rambling. "I found your name open on her browsing history and a confirmation of pregnancy from her doctor on her kitchen table. So, I came here looking for her or you." He ended as he nodded at me.

"It still doesn't explain why you came before dawn?" Ivan asked as he came to stand beside me with a bat in his hand. This was about to get brutal if Mathieu didn't tell the truth.

"Okay, okay," Mathieu spat as he ducked his head down. "I didn't want my boss to know, okay." He glanced up at me. "I can't tell him my sister is pregnant with your baby, now, can I? Just tell me this, are you going to do the right thing here, or are you just keeping her until the baby is born?"

I considered this fact for a moment, feeling my blood rushing to my head. "I guess you can't tell your boss, but you could have waited or left a message instead of breaking in. What kind of man do you think I am?" I asked as my temper flared up. "Did you think she would be here, at a club?" I asked.

Mathieu was about to say something when Ivan brought the bat down on his knee. It made an awful crackling sound as Mathieu let out an eerie screeching sound.

"How dare you insult us that way. Now tell us the truth," Ivan shouted at him.

Looking down, I noticed the blood starting to seep through his pants. Ivan was a big man, and he not only broke his knee but also pierced the skin, it seemed.

Stepping even closer, I took Mathieu by the chin and lifted his head. "Skyler is safe and will stay that way. But you have no business here. Understand."

"No, please," Mathieu begged. "I have to see her, please. Once I know she is safe, then I'll leave you be."

I felt my temper rise further as he would not back off. My free hand formed a fist as I stared into his pathetic eyes.

"I can't trust you. You tried to kill me." I spat as I swung at his face. My knuckles collided with his jaw, filling the room with a loud thud. Mathieu's face swiped sideways as he let out a grunt. Tilting his head, he spat out blood.

Roman followed suit with a couple of hits of his own before I took over again. After a while, Mathieu was spitting blood everywhere and heaving from the punches. His face had started swelling and blood was streaming down the sides.

Stepping back, I took out my handkerchief and wiped my hand. "Look what you have done now," I said, pointing at the blood spatter on my pants. "How am I going to explain this?"

Roman and Ivan laughed as Roman untied Mathieu's hands. "We have a message for your boss," Roman said.

Stepping in beside him, we lifted Mathieu from the chair and moved towards Ivan.

"Messing with us will get him killed and you too," he added as he swung the bat into Mathieu's stomach.

Mathieu folded double in our hands, spitting blood with the last air in his lungs, and we knew it was over. He hung limp in our arms and was battling to breathe. He couldn't even find his feet anymore. Roman and I escorted him outside and into my car. I dropped him on the curb close to the house Roman and Sergei had staked out. They were sure to find him there.

I returned to the club to get clean clothes and discuss the situation with Ivan and Roman. Once we were all on one footing, I headed back to the yacht as the sun was coming up. We would have to get this wedding out of the way soon before things turned upside down.

As I drove back, I noticed my knuckles had some scrapes. Maybe Skyler wouldn't notice, I thought as I pulled in. I had to, he gave me no choice, I told myself.

Her brother had to be taught a lesson. I just hoped in time, she would forgive me. Exciting the car, I considered the fact that she might never even find out about this exchange. After all, by the time she sees him or talks to him, we will be married.

The sun was shining down brightly even though it was still early morning, and I knew it was going to be a hot day. Walking up to the yacht, the guards passed me. "Any issues?" I asked. Both shook their heads in passing, letting me know there was nothing to report.

If Skyler behaved, I might take her to Roman's place for a swim, but let's see how she's been doing this morning. I was sure she wouldn't sleep anymore as it took longer than anticipated. I thought how much trouble she could get in being locked up as I unlocked the door. I didn't stop for breakfast but could always place an order depending on what she wanted.

Stepping in, I was astounded. I didn't even recognize the cabin. Skyler was sitting on the floor beside the bed with her legs pulled up reading. Except for the mess she left, she was also wearing my clothes. She had laid out what appeared to be my entire cupboard on the bed, the floor, and just everywhere. The place was covered in stripes of red, blue, and yellow.

She glanced up as I stood at the door. "Hi, how was your day?" she asked. I could hear a hint of excitement in her voice, which just made the situation worse.

Stepping inside, I slammed the door behind me, as I spoke. "What happened here, Skyler?"

Skyler started giggling, "Isn't it pretty," she said.

"Pretty," I exclaimed. "No, Skyler, this is not; what did you do?"

Chapter 16 - Skyler

I heard footsteps on the deck and knew. Luder had returned. I waited for him to enter. I wanted to see his reaction to the pretty picture I designed.

Stepping inside, he didn't look pleased. His sunny smile evaporated, and his eyes grew large as I asked him about his day.

Slamming the door, he spoke in a serious tone, wanting to know what I had done. Couldn't he see what happened, I thought.

I couldn't help myself as the laugh escaped my mouth, which appeared to have worsened the situation. "Isn't it pretty," I asked, trying to ease the mood.

His reaction was less than charming and made me slightly angry. Rising, I placed the book down on the bed. "I gave the place some color. Plus, your wardrobe. It was way too plain. It was boring." I exclaimed.

He stormed closer, grabbed my arm, and raised his voice as he continued. "No, this is not something you do." Luder pulled me toward the table and pulled the chair out. After forcing me down, he tied my hands and feet.

"Luder," I protested. "Come on, it was a joke."

Leaning closer, he looked into my eyes, "This is no joke."

He grabbed a big black gym bag and started shoving his clothing into it. As he moved from pile to pile, he grumbled.

"Are you leaving?" I asked, feeling a tang of panic entering my mind. I wanted him to let me go not the other way round.

Straiting out, he glared at me. "No, but these will now all have to be washed," he uttered holding the bag out toward me. "You better hope this color comes out." He added as he shoved the bag out the door.

Pacing up to me, he grabbed hold of the chair and leaned in as he spoke. "I thought you would behave and not try to destroy my things, but this is unacceptable. If you want to be treated like a child, I will treat you like one."

Luder stormed out, and after a while, he returned with a bucket and cloth. As he walked drops of water and foam sprinkled over the sides, dropping to the floor. He appeared slightly less angry as he stood in the middle of the room, looking around. I wasn't sure if I should say anything or just let it be.

"Look at this, the walls, windows, cupboards, even the books and shelves are all covered in lines." He said, dropping the bucket and cloth as he folded his hands across his chest.

He took a deep breath and lifted his head back. "No," he breathed out, glancing my way.

I could see the anger had only been hiding as he stared at me. Trying to shift on the chair, I turned my gaze down to the floor. "Sorry," I whispered. This may not have been one of my bright ideas.

"Look, Skyler, look at the mess, even the ceiling has lines across it." Hearing him coming closer, I looked up just as he grabbed hold of the chair again. I flinched as he pulled me and the chair toward him. "How on earth do you think I must get those lines off?" he screamed, narrowing his eyes.

He took hold of my hair and pulled my head back. I blinked as fear settled within me, making me flinch. Luder's expression changed as he stared at me. I knew I deserved everything I got. I only hoped his anger wouldn't drive him to do something extreme.

Letting go, he surveyed the room again. "Now I have to get the cleaners in," he spat as he walked back to the bucket. Turning to me, I noticed his face had softened and so did his tone. "Skyler, what were you thinking hun?"

He took the damp cloth and started wiping down the books and bookshelf. I didn't respond. At that time, it had made a lot of sense to me, but now, I saw the error in my ways. Once the bookshelf was reasonable and the books clean, he wiped down the cupboards and closets. By the time he was done, it was lunchtime.

"Have you eaten this morning?" he asked softly, looking at me. I couldn't get a word out and only nodded my head.

As he moved to the side of the bed, he noticed the half-eaten container on the floor. "Is that all you ate?" he inquired, picking it up. I tried to turn away as he came closer. "Are you hungry?" he asked again, but louder this time.

I turned my head away. "I take that as a no," he said, placing the container on the table. "Well, let me know when you are," he mumbled.

I sat watching him continue to clean as best he could. After changing the bedding, he moved to the kitchen. He wiped down the fridge, cupboard, stove, and counter.

"The ceiling, windows, and floor would have to wait," he said, stepping back outside with the bucket and cloth.

I heard him chucking the water out, and then he spoke to someone called Zoba. I felt sure he was on the phone as I didn't hear anyone else talking. "Only tomorrow," he said, and then there was a pause. "Okay, that will have to do then, we will spend the night with the place as it is. Thank you."

I was wiggling within my constraints as the door slammed shut, and I realized he had returned. "This is not right," I uttered as I calmed down in the chair. "I am hungry, can you untie me so I can eat something?"

Luder grinned at me as he walked over and pulled the chair closer to the bed. He headed to the kitchen and warmed some of the leftover Chinese. Returning, he sat down on the bed before me. Holding out a spoonful, he spoke. "Open wide?"

"No," I protested. "Really, I am not a child, just untie me," I added, turning my head away.

"You act like one, so who am I to say you're not," he retorted, smiling. "Here, you want food, open your mouth. I can feed a child."

I shook my head as he tried to feed me. "Well, I guess you aren't hungry then," he added as he took a bit. "Mmm, this is good. You haven't tried this one, you must taste it," he added holding the spoon out again.

I kept my head sideways and didn't respond, so he placed the container on the bed next to him and closed the lid. "Skyler," he said, tapping me on the knees. Turning back to face him, he continued. "Tell me about this dog you mentioned?"

What was he doing, first, he tied me up, then he wanted to feed me, and now he's asking about Bunny. Well, I can tell him about my dog; maybe he'd realize I need to get home.

"Oh, Bunny, he is a great big ball of love." I started, but as I spoke, I felt my face dropping. "He's all alone at home, and I don't know if Mathieu would bother to check on him."

"You say he's a love ball, really, so he will be friendly with strangers as well?" Luder asked, raising his eyebrows.

Feeling my love for Bunny filling me, my voice was overflowing with compassion as I continued.

"Oh, yes. When he gets excited, he flops around and jumps up and down, smashing into everything at times. If you look into his big eyes long enough, you will be covered in slobbering kisses. He looks aggressive but isn't. I think it's just his size that scares people."

Turning my head toward the window, a tear ran down my cheek. "I miss him so much," I whispered, trying to swallow the heartache that was creeping up my throat.

Luder stood up and walked towards the window. Turning, he leaned back and watched me. I felt his eyes burning through my soul. "You never told me where you live exactly?" he inquired.

Glancing up at him, I exhaled deeply, considering his question. "I promise not to paint your cabin again if you just untie me, I won't be a problem, please Luder. I just want to go home. You can come to visit every day, I'll even introduce you to Bunny and give you a key."

He smiled warmly, "Your address?"

Lowering my head and shaking it, I replied softly, giving him my home address.

Chapter 17 - Luder

I felt sorry for her, she didn't intend to get pregnant, and she didn't think I would hold her. How could she, I mean, she didn't know a thing about me or our family.

She appeared truly sorry, and my heart skipped a beat for a second as I studied her. When she pouted like this, I seemed to be more attracted to her.

An intense feeling of protectiveness came over me. I wanted her to be happy, but it had to be with me. After all, she was carrying my child. As I stood there, my fingers burned to hold her, to touch her silky skin.

If I intended to keep her with me, I would have to make some changes. With this in mind, I decided I would visit her home and meet this, Bunny. Having a dog could possibly be a good thing and it would put a smile back on her face.

"Yes," I uttered as I strolled to her side. Skyler beamed up at me as I untied her. Even though I took away the bounds, it was not why I was agreeing but she couldn't know this. I had made up my mind to collect her dog and give it a try.

Skyler rubbed her wrists where the rope had left small indents before she stood up. Reaching up she placed her arms around my neck. "Thank you, and I am sorry for the mess." She uttered as she gave me a soft hug.

"It's fine," I replied, starting for the door. "The cleaner will be here in the morning. Have the food on the table, and I'll be back a bit later. I have some business to take care of."

Skyler gave me a faint smile, "I thought you were letting me go?" she asked.

"Nope, not a chance hun," I replied as I left and locked the door. I paused a moment thinking of everything that had happened the last couple of weeks. There were so many changes and so many new challenges. But I was confident that we could make it work.

Stepping out into the early afternoon sun I was mission orientated. I knew where I was going and what had to be done. I asked the guards to watch the yacht until I returned. Maybe this time, she would try to burn it down. I considered this as I pulled out and drove to town.

Naw, she wouldn't do that, I thought, smiling at myself in the rearview mirror. The drive to her place took me a bit longer than I expected as the roads were busy this time of the day. Pulling up to the front of her home, I surveyed the area. Everything appeared quiet and normal at first. There were no people or neighbors around.

I left the confines of my vehicle and strolled up the side of the house, trying to see where Bunny was. She said he wouldn't be outside, but I had to be sure. It was a good thing though. As I rounded the side of the house, I saw two men with large guns patrolling the back entrance.

Ducking behind a bush, I waited and watched them. Mathieu most likely had something to do with this, I felt sure of it. He had to know I would be coming here sooner or later. I mean, there was the dog, and she also needed clothing and other things.

Watching them, I wondered if he thought this would be payback, preventing me from entering. After all, I was holding his sister captive, he knew I would have to come to collect some of her things and Bunny.

The men didn't look too pleased to be here. After a couple of minutes, they headed around the side of the house. I could only hope they would stay a while so I could get inside. I neared the door carefully.

Lifting my head over the kitchen windowsill, I saw him. Bunny lay next to the counter. He lifted his head and turned it sideways. Skyler was right, he was adorable. I had to find a way inside that wouldn't attract too much attention, though. Moving slowly to the other corner of the house, I peeked around the corner.

One of the guards stood against the front wall smoking. I couldn't see the other one, but I considered his absence a good thing. He might be walking the front yard for a bit. For a second, I wondered if my car would make them suspicious, but it didn't appear to bother the one smoking. I had parked it halfway before the house next door.

Moving back to the door and window in the kitchen, I tried the knob. But obviously, it was locked. I never even thought of getting her keys. I took out my hunting knife and slid the front end between the window and the frame. I could see the hook was halfway up and it should slip out of the ring with a little push.

I didn't even think there may be an alarm system before unlatching the window. I froze and listened as the knife entered, and the hook fell out of the loop. Breathing out heavily, I was relieved that nothing screamed. So, no alarm. Bunny stood as I pushed the window up.

"Hey, Bunny," I whispered while pulling myself into the window. Bunny gave a loud bark and I looked to the end of the house to see if the guards were coming. But nobody came running around the side of the house. I felt my stomach turning as I glanced back at Bunny.

"Quiet, Bunny," I said, sliding inside. As my feet hit the ground, Bunny started growling. "No, Bunny, I am here to take you to Skyler," I added, kneeling.

Bunny lowered the front part of his body, showing me his teeth. He wasn't pleased to have me here. "Bunny, I am your friend," I whispered, unsure how I would do this. I had not considered any of the factors presenting themselves to me. She said he was a ball of love; this was no ball of love.

I heard the two guards nearing as their voices became louder. "Crap," I whispered. I should have taken them out. What was I thinking entering her home with them still outside? What if they saw the window and called for assistance before I could take them out?

Bunny growled again as I slowly moved towards the door. Watching him, I unlocked the deadbolt and rose against the door peeking through the corner of the window. The guards were only a couple of feet away. I would have to move quickly. Bunny was standing still, growling. I hoped he would stay put as I moved.

Opening the door, I stepped outside. "Hi there, guys," I said as they turned their attention to me. "How are you doing today?" I continued as I closed the door behind me and approached them. They looked confused as they scanned me and then glanced at each other.

"Have you seen Skyler today?" I asked, coming to stand before them.

My fingers itched, holding the nightstick up my sleeve as my hand opened and closed around the handle. I didn't dare take out my gun. Shooting would attract too much attention.

"Where did you come from?" one of the guards asked as he brought the tip of his gun to my chest.

"Whoa, guys," I said, taking hold of the tip with my free hand. "I have keys, and I walk the dog twice a week, what is this all about?"

The guy with his gun pointed at me glanced at the other one. I knew this was it, it was now or never. I couldn't wait for Dumb and Dumber to ask any more questions. I shoved the gun away and swung the nightstick at the guard's head. He was the bigger of the two and I knew I had to make the first hit count.

The gun dropped to the ground as he let go and gripped his head. Blood trickled down the side of his head, and he went down slowly with a soft cry for help. The other guard had lifted his gun as I stepped in and swung at his head.

He pulled back, and my swing missed. I was just relieved that he didn't pull the trigger in his slight confusion. Looking him in the eyes, I realized the situation had dawned on him as clearness entered his face. He stepped back, raising his gun again.

"No," I yelled as I lunged at him. As we collided, I grasped the tip of his gun and pulled down hard. We staggered for a second before we went down. I landed on top of him and didn't wait for a reaction. As I felt my knees touching the ground, I lifted my hands and started beating his face in.

After a couple of seconds, I stopped myself and glared at the lifeless body under me. Blood was dripping off my knuckles. "What the…" I spoke out loud as I stood. Looking around, I spotted an outside tap and quickly rinsed my hands. This was all Mathieu's fault. No one was supposed to be here.

I thought back to the matter at hand as I strolled to the door. As I reached for the handle, I considered pulling the car around. After a second, I decided it would be best as I didn't want to be seen dragging a dog around in broad daylight. Not that I would even know how to do that with a dog his size.

I moved the two men against the house and tied their hands before pulling the car around. I didn't know if the second man was still alive or not, but didn't want to waste time finding out.

Once the car was in place, I opened the door. Bunny was lying down next to his bowls. I hadn't expected him to be so well-behaved. But he started growling again as I stepped inside.

"There, there, Bunny," I spoke as I slowly moved forward. He rose as I came closer and started stepping back. "Bunny," I said as I lowered myself to one knee. "Come on boy, I want to take you to see Skyler." At her name, he stopped growling for a second and turned his head.

This peace didn't last long, though. As I stood and walked forward again, he lunged at me. His growling had turned into something quite scary. I turned as his mouth was about to close around my arm. I grabbed him around the chest and in the back of the neck as we went down together.

As he tried to get to me, I held Bunny to the ground with everything I had. Slobber and foam were coming from his mouth, and I no longer thought of him as a good dog. Although I had entered his home and Skyler had not been here in more than a day. I felt sure he was just very scared and confused.

Picking Bunny up around his waist, I kept a tight grip on the back of his neck. I wasn't about to let him get a bite in. Shoving him into the back seat, I was relieved that I had turned up the window between the back and front. Bunny swung around but I had already closed the door on him.

Standing back, I watch him barking and clawing at the door. "I will most surely need to get the inside redone after this," I said glancing around at the two guards. They appeared to be quiet. I closed the window and grabbed the two bowls, and the bag of dog food before I left the house.

Starting the car, I remembered she needed clothing. Running back in, I grabbed a couple of items and left.

Pulling out of the driveway, I passed a car and two people on the sidewalk. None of them seemed too worried about the barking dog in the back though. I made the drive through town a quick one. Pulling into the parking at the private docks, I pull up as close as possible to the docks where my yacht is parked.

"And this?" one of the guards asked as I stepped out of the car. Bunny was still going on in the back.

"It's a dog," I said as I hastily moved to the yacht.

"Skyler," I practically yelled as I unlocked the door and shoved it open. Skyler was standing just inside, her eyes wide. "Sorry," I mumbled, "I didn't intend to frighten you," I said, taking her hand. "I have something for you," I added, dragging her out and towards the car.

As we came to the edge of the docks where my car was parked, Skyler stopped dead, pulling her hand out of mine. "Bunny," she screamed in a high-pitched voice. Skyler ran to the car and opened the door.

"Slow down," I said from the docks. I wasn't going closer just yet. "He is vicious."

Skyler was down on her knees hugging the big mutt around the neck. Glancing over at me, I noticed the tears running down her cheeks.

I straightened my stance as a sense of accomplishment and pride washed over me. I couldn't help but smile at the two. Bunny was licking her cheek and barking. But this bark was friendly, and his tail swiped left and right like a broom.

It was all worth it. All the hassles of getting Bunny here. It was all worth the trouble he gave me. I was sure her brother wouldn't agree, but that was another day's worries. For now, she was happy.

CHAPTER 18 - SKYLER

Glancing over my shoulder, I saw Luder waiting on the edge of the docks. He was smiling like a Cheshire cat. With tears of joy flowing so strongly, I didn't dare even try to smile at him as I may have burst out in a full crying fit. I held Bunny tight as my mind tried to absorb what had just happened.

This was the last thing I expected from him, especially after this morning's mess. Bunny licked my cheek, his tongue rough and warm, but I didn't mind. Glancing up, I noticed the interior of the back of Luder's car looked even worse than the yacht.

I could only hope he would look past the damage and see the beauty in what he has done. I stayed on my knees, hugging Bunny until I was able to restrain my tears and regain confidence in my voice. My legs felt numb, and my knee ached, but I didn't care.

Standing slowly, I turned and smiled at Luder. "Thank you," I said. Luder nodded his head and waved toward the yacht. I walked toward the yacht with Bunny in tow. "I am sorry for the damage," I added as I passed him.

Bunny followed me willingly into the yacht. Sitting down on the bed, I noticed Luder hadn't followed us to lock the door. "Maybe he will ease up a little now that you are here," I said to Bunny as I rubbed his large head.

After a few minutes, Luder entered carrying the two bowls and dog food. He also had a small bag with what looked like some of my clothing. Maybe I was wrong, he appeared to have a softer side. He cared in his own way, and marrying him may not be as dreadful as I had thought. I will see how he reacts to Bunny though as he can be a handful.

Luder placed the two bowls down next to the table and added food and water. Watching Luder, I wonder if Mathieu would be happy for me if I decided to marry this man. He has shown so much compassion and kindness today, I couldn't deny his good side.

He stood still as Bunny ran over and drank water as if he had done a mile run. Once Bunny was done, he raised his head and sniffed Luder's pants, covering the pipe in slobber. Luder grinned and patted Bunny's head. Yes, I thought as I stood, he was a kind man.

Bunny sat down at his feet as I walked closer. "Luder," I spoke as I came to stand before him, glancing up. His eyes sparkled as his grin turned into a smile.

"Yes," he replied, locking his gaze on me and handing me the bag of clothes.

Suddenly, feeling shy, I looked down and turned from side to side. "I have considered it to great length," I added before looking him in the eyes again. "I have decided to marry you," I concluded. His smile broadened even more as his entire being seemed to glow instantly.

He cleared his throat and stepped around Bunny. "Well then," he said, going down on one knee and looking up at me. "Skyler..." he shook his head and gave a slight laugh. "I don't even know your surname," he added softly.

"Witlock," I replied, giggling. I was filled with excitement as my heart picked up speed. It felt like I was back in high school, and the boy I liked was about to ask me to prom. Yet, this was much bigger than going to the prom.

Luder glanced down, cleared his throat again, and took my hands in his after fumbling with something in his pocket. Looking up this time, I noticed his look had turned serious. Yet, his eyes were soft and compassionate, and so was his voice once he spoke. "Skyler Witlock, will you make me the happiest man on earth and become my bride?" Luder finally said, opening his one hand and holding up a sparkling ring.

I felt the tears burning in my eyes as my heart stopped for a second. Even though I knew he wanted me to marry him, I didn't expect a whole proposal and a ring. It was big, and in the center was a shiny diamond, well, I couldn't be sure, but it looked like one. Surrounding the big one were smaller stones. These were hazel, blue, and gold.

Pulling my hands up to my mouth, I gasped for air. I couldn't contain the tears any longer, they flowed down my cheeks like a river. I was sure the pregnancy hormones had a lot to do with all the crying I'd been doing. But, even though today started out not so good, things were turning out to be good. Everything was so overwhelming. I couldn't get a word out, so I nodded in agreement.

Luder took my hand and slipped the ring on as he came up. It fit perfectly and I couldn't stop staring at it as he pulled me into his warm embrace. I had my hand up in the air to see the ring over his broad shoulders. My face was pulled taught from the smile I couldn't wipe from my face.

I didn't even know why this was making me so happy, but it was. Bunny sat up at the table and growled softly.

"I don't think he approves," Luder said as he stepped to my side and looked at Bunny. "Do you not approve of this dog?" he asked, looking at Bunny and talking slowly.

This made me laugh even though I was crying. "Oh, no, he's just not sure what's happening and why I'm crying," I replied as I called Bunny. He came forward, tail wagging. "There's a good boy," I said, kissing his head. Glancing up at Luder, I felt my heart swell with care.

Luder pulled my phone from his pocket and held it out for me. "Well, here's your phone if you need to call someone," he said.

"Thank you," I said softly as I took the phone. "I might call my brother," I added, watching for his reaction.

Luder looked down at Bunny and spoke as he smiled at me. "Let him know his two men are tied up at your house."

"What did you do?" I asked, astounded at his words.

"Well, I wanted the dog, and they were in my way. I simply tied them up, is all," he added as he turned and headed out.

Bunny whimpered and lay down, covering his eyes with his paws. "Should I believe him?" I asked as I dialed Mathieu's number. "Looking at your reaction, I doubt it, but he did bring you here, so I guess that counts, right?"

Bunny jumped up and loudly barked, making me laugh as I listened to the ringing.

"Skyler?" Mathieu's voice came blaring over the phone. "Skyler, is that you?" he asked,, sounding very concerned.

"Hi, Mathieu," I replied lightly, shaking my head at Bunny.

"Skyler, where are you? I'll come to get you now, just tell me where you are?" he asked hastily.

"Slow down, brother, I'm fine, and who said I want you to come and get me?"

"But I've been looking for you everywhere; I even placed men at your house." Mathieu continued.

"Yeah, about that," I said in a harder tone, remembering Luder's words. "Where do these men come from and who do you really work for?"

Mathieu was silent for a moment. "I... well, I... it is not important. Just let me come get you, and we can talk." He concluded.

"No, Mathieu," I said calmly in an even tone. "I need to know why guards were posted outside my house."

There was a long silence. "Mathieu," I said loudly. As I spoke, I heard the irritation forming in my voice and a hint of anger rising within me.

"I can't explain it over the phone, Skyler," he replied. I could hear the hesitation in his voice.

"So, it's true, you are working for Bratva?" I asked, speaking louder.

Another long silence followed before Mathieu spoke. "It is complicated, I will explain it all to you when I pick you up."

Anger took hold of me before I could even register it, and I was screaming at Mathieu over the phone. "I am fine! I called to let you know I am getting married and will have a baby. But I guess that isn't important either anymore. I don't even know who you are."

"No," Mathieu's voice echoed through the phone. "You can't, please don't do this, let's talk first, please."

I was done talking; he had lied to me, and even with everything Luder had done, he never lied to me. Bunny was barking at me, and my mind wouldn't focus.

"I thought you would be happy for me. But, no, everything in life is always about you, isn't it?" As I spoke, I felt tears of anger and disappointment coming forth. My excitement dwindled as I tried to catch my breath.

91

Mathieu had been very quiet during my outburst, but I knew he was steaming about everything I had said. When he spoke, I could hear the displease in his voice.

"Skyler, it's your hormones talking. Let's sit down and talk it over before you make a mistake."

"No, you don't get to decide for me. Not anymore," I spat at him over the phone. "This is my life and my choice, Mathieu," I added as I stomped my foot on the ground. "You think about your actions and leave my life out of it," I said before chucking the phone at the wall.

Turning, I flopped down on the bed and cried. My tears now flowed freely. I felt Bunny nudging at my feet, but my heart was heavy and frozen in horror. How could he say those things, I thought as my lungs struggled to find air.

I felt a soft, gentle touch on my shoulder. The bed was dented in, and I rolled to the side. Glancing up, I saw Luder had come back in and was sitting next to me on the bed. I flung my arms around him as he pulled me up into his embrace. I needed someone to hold me.

Luder caressed my hair as he held me tight. For the longest moment, we just sat there as I cried. Once I started feeling calmer, I softly pulled back. He cupped my chin and lifted my head.

"Are you okay?" he asked softly.

"I'll be fine, thanks," I said as I turned to look at Bunny. He was sitting quietly now, just staring at us. I rose and went to rinse my face. Returning to the room, I heard Luder on the deck speaking to someone.

Peeking around the door, I saw he was on the phone. I walked to the wall and collected the pieces of my phone. Luder returned as I placed them down on the table.

"We'll get you another one," he commented as he joined me at the table. "Just keep the sim card and chuck the rest."

Pulling me into his arms again, he whispered, "I have a surprise for you,"

Looking up at his expression made me wonder as he looked like a child who had just won a prize. "Really," I asked lightly pushing him away.

"Bring Bunny, we're going for a drive," Luder said as he walked to the door, smiling back at me.

I called Bunny and followed him to the car. We pulled out and headed to town with Bunny securely in the back.

Chapter 19 - Luder

Skyler was staring out the window as we drove, and I could see she was still upset. Wanting to make her feel better, I decided to take her out. We couldn't go to a restaurant with Bunny along, but I called Ashan and asked him to make arrangements for me at Roman's place. I called Roman first, though, to make sure it would be fine for us to come over.

Roman sounded as eager as Ashan when I told him what I wanted to do. Being part of a big family has a lot of benefits, and if anyone could pull off what I wanted, those two could.

Bunny sat quietly in the back as we drove. There was no more aggression or any sign of anger in him. Well, none that was visible. Glancing at Skyler, I felt the blood in my veins starting to boil. She was an amazing woman I had to admit. Getting to know her over the last couple of days has been an experience and a half.

I felt good that she was the one carrying my child. Who knows what kind of woman I would have ended up with and if I ever would have settled. She was intelligent, kind, loving, and very easy on the eyes. I grinned as we pulled up to Roman's place, and Skyler gasped.

"Where are we?" she asked as the large gates opened, revealing the house within its walls.

"This is my cousin's place," I remarked casually, parking by the fountain.

Skyler looked dazzled as she shook from excitement. Bunny let out a long howl. "It's so beautiful," Skyler added, smiling from ear to ear.

It was amazing how easily she got excited. I could only hope she would not have an issue with what was coming. Getting out, I quickly moved to open her door. Holding out my hand for her, I saw Ashan, Roman, and Karine coming down the stairs to meet us.

Skyler clung to my arm as she noticed them. "Who did you say stays here?" she asked, glancing up at me.

Opening the back door for Bunny, I replied softly. "I told you we were coming to my cousin's place." Bunny jumped out and went straight to Skyler's side. "Come on, there are some people I want you to meet," I added as I started walking with her around the car. Having her on my arm, I walked proudly.

After introducing Skyler to the family present, we moved around the house to the back. As we went, I heard her gasp at this and then that. She was entranced by the time we got to the backyard. Bunny followed quietly, sniffing everywhere.

At the back, the tables were halfway made up, and more of the family were waiting for us. There were more tables than usual, all covered in white and gold cloth. After the introductions, Karine and Irina took Skyler inside. I followed them into the kitchen.

"Skyler," I said as Karine gave me a nod. She turned and stared questioningly at me with her eyebrows lifted. "If you want, we can get married right now. Everything is prepared."

She glanced at the two women waiting for her and back at me. "Right now?" she asked, astounded. I nodded in agreement and smiled. Skyler looked at Bunny, who had followed us inside, before nodding in agreement. "This is very sudden, but I guess we can."

Leaning closer, I kissed her cheek before she was taken upstairs to get ready. Stepping back outside, I was just in time to assist with the last details. The archway went up quickly, we scattered the yard with rose petals in gold, silver, white, and red color. Sergei quickly discussed the ceremony with me before Ivan came over and asked me her full name. He would be marrying us.

As we placed flowers, wine, and glasses on the tables, more of the family arrived. The woman assisted either in the kitchen with the food or outside with decorations. Roman stood by his bar and gave orders to the younger men.

Next to the bar, a stage assembled practically out of thin air. This was turning out to be much bigger than I could ever have imagined. By the time everything was in place, the yard was full to breaking point. Samantha headed inside to see if Skyler was ready while I stood waiting by the flower arch with Ivan, Ashan, and Roman.

Everyone was talking, and the atmosphere was joyful. My stomach made a strange turn as the wedding march started playing. Silence fell over the backyard as all attention turned to the doorway.

I held my breath as Samantha and Irina came out first, and then Karine followed before Skyler appeared. She looked like a princess stepping out of a fairytale. She was glowing, and I gasped for air. She took my breath away as she walked toward me. I had no idea where everything came from in such a short time, but I thought whoever got the dress had style.

Skyler's hair was pinned up with a couple of locks falling from the crown to frame her face. There was only a tinge of make-up and the dress. Oh, the dress highlighted every perfectly formed feature. I felt my mouth hanging open as Ashan pushed my chin back up.

He leaned toward me and whispered, "Really, bro, I am sure you've seen more of her than this."

Glancing at him, I felt a twinge in my arm to just smack him but smiled at him instead. "Yes, but she… she looks amazing at the moment don't you think?"

Ashan just shook his head. As the other women joined us and moved to the side, I took Skyler's hands. "You're shining brighter than the evening star on a clear night," I whispered as we came to stand before Ivan.

Skyler beamed at me and then looked at Ivan. Feeling the smile on my face pulling every muscle, I tried to pull my face right and nodded at Ivan to continue. I have never felt so entranced by anyone before. This was all new to me, but I liked the way she made me feel. She gave me strength and a calmness that no one else could.

This, like everything in our lives, was no ordinary wedding ceremony as we never tend to stick to the rules of society. Ivan started by welcoming everyone and announcing the reason for our gathering. He spoke about the importance of family and how growing a strong family keeps everyone happy and safe.

As he went through the wedding vows, I noticed a tear strolling down Skyler's cheek. My heart ached for her, knowing that she had no family present. Yet, I knew my family would make up for her loss. Just before Ivan could conclude the ceremony, a string of gunfire filled the air.

Turning toward the house, tables were being shoved over for shelter, and the family pulled their guns aiming in one direction. Karine, Irina, and Sam had already pulled Skyler to them. Glancing around, I felt relieved as they were safely behind the wall leading down to the pool area.

I did not bring my guns as I didn't expect any trouble here. Looking at the house, I saw Mathieu standing in the doorway. He was surrounded by men, presumably from Domique's Bratva.

Stepping forward, Mathieu moved toward me. "What is this, Mathieu?" I asked, feeling all eyes on us. I knew I was an open target, but no one would be standing if they took a shot at me.

"I just want Skyler back," he replied, aiming at my chest. I had to give it to the man; he had balls. Coming here and requesting such a thing.

Glancing over my shoulder, I nodded as this day was about to turn upside down. I stepped closer to Mathieu, lowering my voice as I spoke. "She is part of our family now; I think it is best if you and your men leave now."

Mathieu laughed, lifting his head, a horrid taunting kind of noise came from his mouth. "Oh, it's not that simple, you know," he replied as his laugh subdued. "She is my sister and I have a duty to talk sense into her." Glancing around, he called out to her, "Skyler, Skyler, come out here now."

"A duty," I heard Skyler say loudly behind me. Turning, she was briskly walking toward us. It looked like steam was coming from her ears. By the expression on her face, I knew she was not about to go quietly. Knowing she wanted to be here filled my being with a passionate need to protect her.

As Skyler moved in beside me, I grabbed her around the waist to prevent her from moving into Mathieu's grip. "Slow down, hun," I spoke gently as she gave me a deadly look.

"He has no right over me; I am my own person, and he can't tell me what I can or cannot do." Skyler spat over her shoulder at Mathieu. "I don't even know who you are anymore," she added.

Turning her around and back towards the family, Karine was there to take her back to safety. Skyler went with her without hesitation.

"You heard the lady. Please leave now," I said, turning my back to him and following the women.

"Skyler," Mathieu called. "You know this isn't right."

Just before the two women reached the wall, a shot went off. I felt the bullet grazing my ear as it passed my head.

"Mathieu," Skyler screamed as she turned. Karine and Irina grabbed hold of her and pulled her behind the wall. "What are you doing," her voice echoed from the cover of safety.

Wiping my ear, I felt the hot blood trickling from the scrapped skin. My blood boiled as I turned to face Mathieu. Ivan, Ashan, Roman, and Sergei all stepped up beside me. Their guns were aimed at Mathieu.

"This is not the time or place to make your mark, Mathieu," I spat as I stormed forward. "Leave or die here today," I uttered as I shoved him backward. My anger could no longer be controlled. Who did he think he was, coming here on this day?

He had caused her enough pain, and I wouldn't let it continue. Mathieu struggled to stay upright as he staggered backward. I continued to move in and shoved him again. "Make your choice," I said loudly, lifting my hands as he fell back. His men had their weapons lifted and aimed at me.

"Look around," I screamed at them. "Do you think this is a fight you can win?"

There was a murmuring in the air as the men whispered. Two came to Mathieu's side and helped him up. He dusted himself off before looking me in the eye. "This is not over," he said, spitting on the ground before my feet.

"No, I expect it isn't," I replied harshly.

Waving his hand through the air, the men cleared the area as quickly as they came. Turning back, the entire family stood watching me. "Well, this day didn't go as planned," I said, walking to Skyler. "We have to go, this isn't over," I added, taking her hand.

Dusk appeared to also have arrived without notice. "It was getting too dark to be safe out in the open," I said, turning to the family. Once we greeted everyone, we headed back to the yacht.

Skyler sat in silence all the way back. She stared out the window and I wondered what she was thinking. She was still wearing the dress. But my main concern was to get her back to the safety of the docks without any other issues on our way. Roman had sent two cars with us as escorts, just in case.

Pulling in, I noticed the guards were already doubled in numbers inside and strolling up and down the perimeter. Roman had surely called and informed them of the situation.

CHAPTER 20 - SKYLER

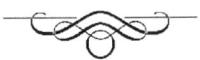

My mind kept repeating the events, and I didn't even notice we had pulled into the parking area at the docks. I was startled when Luder opened the door and held out his hand. Glancing around, I saw there were a lot more guards than normal. I didn't care as my entire being felt tired.

All I wanted was a bed to lie down on. To close my eyes and forget. I felt nauseated, and my stomach was a tight ball. My eyes burned, and my skin felt itchy as I stepped out of the car. Today, my emotions took a rollercoaster ride. There were so many ups and downs that my mind seemed unable to cope with all the information.

Luder let Bunny out the back, and he happily trotted to the yacht and sat waiting for us. I held onto Luder's arm tightly as my legs felt like Jello, and I wasn't sure I would make the trip up the docks and into the yacht.

I felt my legs give way as we walked up the three steps. Luder reacted quickly, before I could hit the deck, I was hoisted into his warm embrace. Flinging my arms around his neck, I closed my eyes, feeling relief wash over me. I could hear his heartbeat, and it was soothing. He was so gentle; the whole family stood up for and protected me.

For the first time in my life, I felt part of something bigger. Maybe it was just the overwhelming emotions of the day. But I felt safe with them. They were not even close to the stories I had heard. Maybe some of the other Bratva, like the ones Mathieu worked for, maybe, they were the bad ones. But Luder's family, the Morozovs, were good people.

Luder placed me down on the bed and sat beside me, holding my hand. "Skyler," he whispered. "Are you okay?"

I turned and looked into his incredible eyes, "I will be." I replied softly. "I just can't…" I felt the tears forming as I tried to explain how I felt about Mathieu. But the lump in my throat threatened to tear through it, so I stared out the window.

"It's okay," Luder responded, rubbing my back. "Can I get you some water or something to drink?"

He was so understanding, kind, and soft. I just wanted to hug him for everything. Nodding, I tried to smile at him, but my face felt stiff, and my mouth didn't want to move. Glancing around as he moved to the fridge, I saw Bunny patiently sitting by the end of the bed. I lightly tapped next to me, and he jumped up and cuddled into my arm.

"Oh, no, my place has been taken," Luder remarked as he came back. "Well, I need to make a call anyway; here's some juice." He said placing the glass down on the bedside table. He glanced back as he left the cabin to go outside, pulling the door only halfway closed.

Hugging Bunny, I allowed my feelings to pour out and sobbed into his coat. "Oh, Bunny, how could Mathieu do this? I don't even know who he is," I whispered between sobs. Bunny, licked my arm that was holding him.

I cried for a long time as my heart was broken into pieces. I wondered how long Mathieu had been in this line of work and how I didn't even notice. My world had turned upside down since meeting Luder for the first time. I could only hope I was doing the right thing for Bunny, the baby, and me.

Everyone was so supportive and nice, especially Luder. Drying my eyes and sitting up, I thought about his kindness. My heart stirred as my mind dwelled on everything we had been through. "This marriage might not only be for the child's sake," I whispered to Bunny. I felt a pulling within as I thought of spending the rest of my life with him.

Smiling softly at Bunny, I wondered if I was falling in love. It could be my emotional state, but my feelings toward Luder were changing. The more I pondered on everything, the more I felt sure of it.

I had just finished the juice and was getting up to rinse the glass when he came back in. Feeling better, I gave him a warm smile. "You got your business done?" I inquired as he sat down at the table.

101

"Yes, thank you," he replied, smiling. "Are you feeling better?"

I nodded and joined him at the table. "Luder," I said, glancing at Bunny, still lying on the bed.

Luder lifted his hands as he spoke. "No, there is no need for any explanations, he has made his choice." Clamping his hands together, he continued. "Let's not ponder on things. But we will have to keep an eye out now."

"Yes, I guess we would have to," I said, reaching over the table and taking his hand. "Thank you."

Luder caressed my fingers. He placed his other hand over mine, his touch was soft and warm. "This is one of the reasons why I don't trust people," he said softly. "Everyone is out to get you, you know."

Smiling softly at him, I replied with care. "No, Luder, I don't think everyone is out to get you." Leaning in closer, I pushed my lips out at him in a pout, making him smile. "Some people just get lost," I concluded.

His smile faded, and his eyes narrowed. "I don't think so; people make their own choices in life," he said, squeezing my hand. "I had this girl…," he said as he sat back in his chair and stared at the ceiling. "Family is important to me, and dishonesty is the one thing I can't take in this world."

Luder breathed in deeply and exhaled slowly as he focused on me. "I grew up in Russia but have been here with the family since I turned nineteen. I had a girl back there, my high school sweetheart."

There was a flickering in his eyes as he pushed his hand through his short hair. "I thought she was the one. But, after finding her with my best friend, I knew no one could ever be trusted."

He took a deep breath and looked away. "It was our last year of high school; graduation was around the corner. She was a cheerleader, you know. One of the most beautiful women I have ever seen." Taking another deep breath, he focused back on the ceiling. I felt a pull inside. I wanted to reach out and let him know it was okay. "We were going to get married right after graduation and she was to come live with me here in America." He added after a short pause.

He shook his head before glancing at me. "If it wasn't for Ashan," he spoke in a low voice. I could hear the pain he held inside. "Well, I might have done something to her and my best friend that I would have regretted for the rest of my life. Instead, I boarded the plane alone, lost for a while as I tried to settle here. From there on out, I stuck with number one. I truly believed that she was the one. I never found love like that with anyone else."

Looking me in the eye as he finished made my heart bleed for him, so much pain at such a young age. "Luder, I'm so sorry," I started saying when he picked up his hand and held it up, indicating I could wait.

"I don't want your sympathy," he said, breathing out slowly. "I want you to know why I do things a certain way and why I find it hard to trust people."

I nodded and gave him what I hoped was a comforting smile.

"After coming here to work alongside Sergei, I discovered that I had a wild streak, as the family calls it," he said, pulling his lips up to one side. "I am known to them as a ladies' man and the go-to guy for sorting things out."

At this, I pulled back slightly. Luder looked at me and leaned in. "I'm not, but that is what people think," he whispered. "You see, I had to take on a no-care attitude to protect myself from the same kind of loss. However…"

Thinking about the recent events with Mathieu, I knew what he meant. But Mathieu is my family, and in time, I will be able to forgive. "Yes," I prodded.

"I have done things that could make today look like child's play," he said. "However, with you and our child," he smiled at me as he rose from the table. "I am willing to put it all aside and give you my all," he added as he walked around to me, holding his hand out.

Placing my hand in his, Luder pulled me up and held me tight. "I promise not to lie to you or ever let anything happen to you or our child," he whispered, kissing my cheek. "Until now, Ashan has been the only one able to control me in an outrage. But you seem to have the same hold."

I embraced him tightly. He made me feel safe, and I needed that more than anything right now. We stood for a bit, just holding each other. After a while, he pulled back slightly and lifted my head in his hand.

"I don't think we even ate with all that happened," he commented.

Shaking my head, I replied, "No, we didn't, but I don't really feel hungry."

"Even so, you must have something, I have some fruit, how about a salad?" he asked, walking to the fridge. Luder took out some berries, apples, and other fruit and made a salad with some cream added.

I have to admit, once I started eating, I could feel I was a bit hungry. After we ate, we took turns showering and got ready for bed. Luder held me in his arms with Bunny on the floor beside us. Sleep came quickly as my body relaxed.

Chapter 21 - Luder

Waking to gunfire was not what I wanted. Glancing at the clock on the wall, I noticed it was only two am. But I knew gunfire when I heard it. The noises outside became louder, and I could hear people screaming at each other.

The hand radio I had placed on the charger a week back started blaring. At first, it was only static. Getting up slowly so as not to wake Skyler, I moved to pick it up and dialed down the volume a bit.

"Who's got the east side?" a voice screamed over the radio. I glanced back at Skyler, who was still sleeping, I noticed Bunny was sitting next to the bed with his ears lifted, making soft growling sounds. I placed my finger over my mouth and made a 'shhh' sound for him to quiet down. At least with him there, I felt sure no one would simply be able to take her.

Bunny lay back down as I left the cabin. Stepping out, I heard one of the guards calling for assistance by the gate. The air was filled with a strong sulfur smell and dust from all the gunfire. Something was wrong here, but I didn't know what was happening. Stepping up to the docks, I saw headlights on the gate from about six cars and men running in all directions.

In the distance behind the gate, I heard Mathieu calling for the men to move through the gates and search all the yachts. I had to get Skyler out of here and quickly. "Protect the gate," I spoke over the radio.

"Yes, we will do so, boss," one of the guards spat back, sounding quite out of breath.

My yacht had an open line to sea but took a couple of minutes to get in gear, and once I started the engine, they would know where to go. "Can some of you find your way to two or three of the other yachts and start their engines?" I inquired over the radio. "I need to scramble our location."

There were a couple of seconds of silence, even the gunfire seemed to have seized as I waited in anticipation for a reply. "Yes," came three voices after each other, blaring through the radio.

"Thanks, men, see you on the other side," I said as I headed back inside. Looking at the cabin door, I turned on the engine and waited for her to kick in. I heard two other yachts roar as their motors kicked in and knew it was time.

Turning the steering, I pushed the throttle up and allowed her to take off. As she moved out of the docks, the gunfire became much clearer. They were moving in quickly. Some of the bullets hit the control room windows and others somewhere on the outer sides before I heard Mathieu screaming at the men. "Don't shoot the boat; my sister could be on it."

I was glad we had installed bulletproof windows and sides. My boat was safe even if they shot at us. But Mathieu didn't know that. I only hoped the men could keep them off the others.

Maneuvering her through the cove, I left the docks and entered the open waters, picking up speed. Once we were out of the cove, I called Sergei and Ashan to inform them of the developments. They assured me their men would assist in the docks within minutes.

Hearing a banging on the cabin door, I looked back at the docks. Feeling sure we were out of danger, I turned off the engine and allowed her to drift. "I'm coming, Skyler," I called out, walking to the cabin door. With the engine off, I could hear Bunny howling softly from inside.

As I opened the door, Skyler came barging out. "What the hell," she spoke in an angry tone seemingly to be bouncing everywhere. Bunny was on her heels and almost jumped me over.

"Slow down, hun," I said pushing Bunny back gently. "I see you haven't found your sailor feet yet," I added, grabbing her. "We were being attacked and I had to get us out."

Skyler's eyes widened as I spoke. "What? By whom?" she asked, glancing around. "What are we doing out in the ocean?" she added, pulling out of my arms. But it seemed she had to bend over and push both her arms out to the sides for balance.

Taking hold of her again and pulling her into my arms, I walked back into the cabin. "It's okay, we are safe out here," I replied as we sat down on the bed. "I take it you've never been out to sea?" I inquired, smiling at her now pale complexion.

Skyler shook her head slowly from side to side as she placed her hands over her mouth. "I'll get a bucket," I said as I moved to the cupboard in the corner. Returning, I handed her a small bucket I kept for when friends got seasick.

"We'll head back in a while. I'm just waiting for word from Sergei or Ashan. Just sit still, it will pass soon," I added, walking back out to grab the radio. Dialing the volume back up a bit, I heard Ashan talking to the men. He had arrived so we could go back to shore, as I was sure the situation was contained.

Starting the engine and pushing the throttle, I called back to Skyler. "Sit tight, hun, we are going back in." I heard her mumbling something before she started upchucking. I took the turn slowly and proceeded back through the cove. As I docked the yacht, the area was quiet.

On the docks stood Ashan and Sergei with our men all over the place. There were a couple of casualties, but it could have been worse. They were glad to see Skyler and me safe. "Good thinking," Sergei said as I chucked the rope at them.

"I wouldn't have gone but I needed to keep Skyler safe," I replied, holding out my hand to Ashan. "Thank you again."

Sergei nodded his head. "I'm heading home, you stay safe now. We'll make a plan once everyone else is up, okay?" he added before walking off. Ashan and I stood watching as Sergei waved his men and drove off.

Ashan's men were assisting mine in assessing the damage and get the ones that needed medical treatment to a hospital. "One of my men found this," Ashan said, holding out a paper for me to look at.

It appeared to be a segment of a brief. There were three pages, a bit dusty, crumpled, and torn, but I could make out about half the content. It contained photos of some family members and notes on Skyler and me. Images of her and Bunny and a part that stated their plans.

This last part, however, was the most damaged. We could make out the times for tonight's attack, though.

107

Hearing movement behind us, we both swung around, and Ashan even pulled his gun. "Hey," Skyler said, bringing her hands up in front of her face. Bunny started growling beside her as I placed my hand on Ashan's gun and pushed it down.

"So sorry, I'm sorry," Ashan blurted out, placing his gun back in its holster. "You startled us."

"It's okay," I added, stepping closer to her. "Quiet down, Bunny," I said, rubbing his head before placing my arm around Skyler. Her touch was so light it sent a shiver down my spine. Yet, it was warm and welcoming.

"I hope you're feeling better, hun. You can go back to bed," I added, kissing her forehead.

"Feeling better but not going back to bed," she said, smiling at me. "I was thinking breakfast?"

"Yes, yes, yes," Ashan chanted, his smile lighting up his deep blue eyes. One was more an icy blue and the other was just a deep blue, unlike mine, which were two different colors.

"Who said you're invited," I taunted as we moved back inside.

Skyler stepped out of my hold and walked in before us. "You can't expect a man to leave his home this time of the morning and not give him some kind of reward," Skyler spoke, looking back at me over her shoulder.

Ashan and I both burst out laughing. "She's a keeper," he added as we sat at the table while Skyler started breakfast.

She smiled warmly as she made some toast, bacon, and eggs. I wasn't even aware I had so much food available, but somehow, she made a great breakfast. Even Bunny had some bacon with us, as there was more than we expected.

After we ate, Ashan thanked her for the meal and left. We would meet up a bit later at Ivan's club. Once we were all washed and dressed, we also headed out. The sun had lazily made its way up and was shining brightly. We took Bunny with us as I didn't want to take any chances on her brother returning.

The club was still closed for normal business, and we had to enter through the side doors. We were surprised by all the family. It seemed everyone was gathered there.

The inside of the club had been changed so much that I didn't even recognize the place. It was like we stepped into a storybook. Small lights hung from the ceiling in rows, casting a golden glow over everything. There were rows of glittering stones and some with flowers. It was everywhere.

Skyler let go of my arm and turned in a circle, staring at the magnificent display in awe. "It's so romantic," she said, looking at me.

The tables were all lined up on the two sides of the floor. On each was a platter with food, champagne, plates, and glasses. At the front of the stage was a flower arch with Ivan waiting for us. "What is this," Skyler inquired looking around.

Sergei stepped forward, out of the family, grouped to the side, holding a black clothing bag. "We thought it best to get it done if you want?" he said, handing over the bag.

Beaming, Skyler slid across the floor, taking the bag from him. "The other one is still back at the yacht," she added, grinning. He nodded, and she followed the woman to the back to get changed.

Ivan waved us to the bar as he walked over smiling. "We weren't sure if she would agree, but we are glad for you," he said, handing me a shot. My heart filled with love for my family. It was a bit strange to see Ivan like this, though. I had become used to his grins but a full smile.

Sergei held his glass up and turned to me, grinning. "Here's to the rest of your life, Luder."

We cheered and downed the vodka shot. "Don't get me wrong," I said, tapping my glass on the counter before placing it down. "I was just as surprised. I didn't expect this after the recent events. But I must thank you all."

As we finished our second shot, music started playing. "It's time to get married," Ivan said, returning to the flower arch.

Ashan and Sergei stood with me as Roman led Skyler through the tables. I couldn't help the grin forming as Skyler walked towards me. She looked stunning, her beauty undeniable.

The white lacy dress sat tight over her breasts and flared out as it went down her legs. There were two slits up the sides which allowed her legs to move through and be seen as she walked.

Her hair was done up like before, and the golden crown made her sparkle. I felt like the luckiest man on earth as she placed her hand in mine, and we turned to face Ivan. This time, we would get it right.

"Seeing as we are gathered for a second time, let's skip the first part," Ivan announced, winking at Skyler. She softly nodded in agreement, looking very pleased.

Ivan glanced around the room. "We're gathered here for the marriage of Skyler and Luder. Is there anything the two of you want to say?" he asked, looking from her to me.

Skyler looked down and smiled. "I would never have imagined us here." She started before looking into my eyes. "I am glad it is you even though I still don't truly know you. You opened my eyes to a whole other world. You give love and kindness new meaning."

The room was filled with giggles and some murmuring as no one here knew me in this way. Clearing my throat, I surveyed the room, and everyone quieted down.

"Skyler," I said, a lump suddenly forming in my throat. "Our meeting wasn't intentional or planned, but you make me happy. You give me a strength I have never felt before. I want to thank you for deciding to stay and take a chance on me. I vow to do all in my power to make you both happy."

Skyler squeezed my hand as a tear ran down her cheek, and Bunny howled. "Oh, yes, the three of you," I said, grinning down at him.

This brought laughter to the room as Bunny howled harder. I felt at ease knowing the atmosphere was relaxed. Cheers filled the room, and Ivan had to raise his hand for silence to continue.

"Well then," Ivan said, bringing everyone's attention back to us. "With all said, please exchange rings." Roman handed me a ring which I slipped onto Skyler's finger. She turned to Karine, who handed her a black platinum wedding band. Skyler's face had streaks through the make-up as her tears rolled down her cheeks.

Ivan waited until we had slipped the rings on before continuing. "I now pronounce you husband and wife. You may kiss the bride."

I placed my hands on Skyler's neck and pulled her closer for a kiss. Our lips met with more passion than I have experienced. Her lips were soft and warm. Her mouth opened invitingly. It sent vibrations down my body as parts of me started waking but I couldn't seem to be able to pull away. Why her kiss affected me this way, I didn't understand but it felt right.

Skyler pulled back after a while, softly gasping for air as she flung her arms around me and hugged me tightly. "Thank you," she whispered before we turned to the family.

The room filled with voices as everyone cheered while we walked to the first table for a champagne toast. The family took turns congratulating us as they moved to the tables set out for them. Roman handed us an envelope, which was a gift from the family for our honeymoon.

"There's no rush," he said as I slipped it into my breast pocket. "It's valid for a year. However, I do think the sooner you go the better." He added, tapping his stomach. Glancing at Skyler, I smiled, he was so right.

Ivan put music on for those who wanted to dance. But the first song was only for us to have an opening dance.

Skyler moved with me easily enough and it turned out to be a lot of fun. We matched in so many other ways, I thought as she swirled in my arms. Her whole being shone and sparkled as she flowed across the floor. I felt my heart skipping a beat a couple of times as our eyes met. She was more than perfect. She was the one.

Shortly before opening time for the club, we all pitched in and started cleaning the place up. Well, not quite cleaning, but we at least moved the tables back and removed the plates, glasses, and other décor.

As we were leaving, there was a loud noise from the back of the club. Smoke filled the room within seconds. I grabbed Skyler's hand as the side door and front doors swung open.

Flames lapped at the kitchen door as another explosion rocked the club. "What the hell," Ivan shouted from somewhere behind us. "You're messing with the wrong family," he added as everyone gathered in the middle of the room.

The men surrounded the women with our guns aimed at all directions. "Come on, cowards," Roman shouted at the figures standing at the doors.

We couldn't make a move with so much smoke and would have to wait for it to start clearing before moving forward or out. The figures in the doors moved in and out, we weren't sure what they were doing. We watched them intently, waiting for them to come closer or make a move.

Ivan and two cousins proceeded slowly toward the kitchen to put out the spreading fire while we held our circle. Once the smoke started clearing, we moved towards the doors. As we went, we kept an eye on our surroundings, expecting men to jump at us.

But the place was empty, the parking area as well except for some of the staff that had started arriving. We scanned the surrounding area, the buildings, and down the street. But just as they came, they went.

Back inside, they had managed to douse the fires completely, but the kitchen was about destroyed. The family was distraught, and I didn't blame them. "This was them," Ivan yelled, slamming the kitchen door.

"We'll clean up," Roman said, touching my shoulder. "You two get out of here." I felt the same; leaving would be best for now.

Sergei and Ashan nodded at me across the floor as I lifted my hand. Taking Skyler around the waist, I headed for the car.

"No," she started saying. I squeezed her and shook my head.

"Not now, hun," I replied, opening the car door for her.

Chapter 22 - Skyler

I wanted to stay and offer support or help with something, but Luder insisted we leave. As we drove off, I looked back, very upset and shocked at what had happened. Another day and place were ruined by my brother and his boss. I would have to put a stop to this soon.

"I can't understand why we had to leave," I spat at Luder as he took the highway down to the coast.

Hearing the irritation in my voice, Bunny started barking in the back. I could see this was bothering Luder as he kept giving Bunny scrunched-up glares over his shoulder as we went.

"Bunny, quiet down," I spoke softly so he could calm down.

"There are enough people to assist them," he replied flatly, not glancing my way.

Studying the bright morning, I couldn't understand why Mathieu would get involved with the kind of people he currently worked for. I had to find out what happened, and how he got caught up in all of this. We weren't raised violently, our mother was most likely fuming in her grave, rest her dear soul.

Our father, well, who knew what he would have thought. He didn't even bother sticking around for us, so his reaction wouldn't matter. Feeling my mood dropping further, I shook my head to clear these evil thoughts.

Now that we were married, I wondered if Luder would let me leave the docks. I needed to collect some of my things, but I also had to see

Mathieu. Somehow, I needed to put a stop to this insanity. Once Mathieu knew we were married, he could stop this war.

Pulling into the docks, I noticed there were more men than usual. "Do you think they will come back?" I asked as Luder stopped the car. The place was crawling with guards, it made me a little uncomfortable.

"Not sure, but they know where we are and after today…" He looked out over the ocean as he spoke and then went silent. He seemed far away in a world of his own for a moment as his eyes appeared to go blank.

"Luder," I whispered, gently touching his hand.

"Yes, sorry," he replied, glancing my way. "Let's get inside, okay?" he added as he got out.

Bunny and I followed him back inside. He put the kettle on and took out two cups. "You want something to drink, some tea, water, juice?" he asked politely, trying his best to give me a comforting smile, but I could see through the plastered-on joy.

"No, I'm fine, but…" I said and waited for a reaction.

Luder looked straight at me. "But?" he questioned.

Swinging from side to side, glancing at my feet, I asked him straight out. "Will it be possible for me to collect some of my things from my home?"

He was quiet for a while as he prepared some coffee for himself. Once it was made, he sat down at the table, staring into the mug. I sat down opposite him and waited patiently.

I knew I was asking a lot. Yet, considering all things, it wasn't that big of an ask, was it? After an awkward silence, he nodded but didn't look at me. I wished I knew what he was thinking.

Excited to get home, I jumped up. "Thank you, may I take the car?" I asked.

Luder looked up, "No, I'll have someone drive you. You know it's not safe."

I wasn't pleased but accepted it. At least he wasn't accompanying me, and I was being allowed out. I would find a way to slip the guard to see Mathieu. Nodding, I turned and headed for the door. "Can I leave Bunny?" I asked as I stopped and looked back at him.

Luder held his mug in both hands, lifting it and blowing steam from the top. He was far away in thought, and I couldn't help but feel my heart aching for him. He nodded slowly. I walked back and kissed him on the cheek before leaving.

Outside, a driver was standing ready by the car and a guard. I wondered if Luder somehow knew I would want to visit my home. They appeared to have been waiting for me.

However, this wasn't important. I gave the driver my address and got in the car. Driving into my neighborhood, I noticed many of the homes still looked the same, nothing had changed.

I haven't been gone that long, but it felt like an eternity. It was comforting being back. I asked the driver to pull around back as I needed to pack and collect some of my things. Spotting behind the house was easier, yes, but it also gave me an opportunity.

Once we stopped, I told the driver and guard they could wait outside. Entering the house, the kitchen was a mess. "How did Luder get in?" I spoke to the room as I looked around.

Checking my watch, I knew that there wouldn't be time to fuss around. Grabbing a suitcase from the bedroom closet, I threw some of my favorite clothes in and dragged them to the back door.

The driver took everything I brought out and loaded it in the boot. I collected my old cell phone from the bedside table and sent Mathieu a message. I asked him to meet me in the park in about half an hour. This ought to give me enough time to slip out and get to the park, as it wasn't far.

Once everything I wanted to take was loaded, I stood looking at my small house. Carefully, I walked through each room. I am going to miss the evenings with Bunny, watching movies, and having hot chocolate with marshmallows. I didn't know Luder's plans, but we had to discuss it. I wasn't about to raise a child on a yacht, and I felt sure he wasn't going to move in with me. In time, I would probably sell the house or rent it out.

Glancing through the kitchen window, I saw the guard pacing up and down the backyard. The driver was leaning against the car. I quickly walked to the front door and softly unlocked it. Walking down the short footpath, I stopped on the sidewalk and glanced back. There was no alarm or movement, which was good.

Feeling panicked, I quickly walked to the corner of the block. There was still no sign of the guard or anyone for that matter. Feeling confident I was out of sight, I strolled quickly to the park a couple of blocks away.

Entering the park, I checked my watch. It was a little early, but not much. I walked to the middle and sat on the bench where we typically met up. The park was quiet, not the usual busy hive of people and dogs. "It is a weekday," I said as I looked around.

Shivering as something crawled up my pine, I wondered if this was a good idea. Standing, I saw Mathieu appearing to the west of me, cautiously looking around as he came closer. "I'm alone," I called out as I stood waiting. "Did you really think I would bring someone else here?" I continued as he pulled me into a light hug.

I felt hurt that he would even consider such a thing. He was my brother, and no matter who I was with, I would never allow anyone to harm him. Mathieu gave me a small grin and sat down. His attention seemed to be somewhere else as he kept glancing around.

"Mathieu, what have you gotten yourself into?" I inquired as I joined him on the bench. "Look at the mess you've made lately."

He looked at me as if the cat had dragged me in. "Me," he spat. "What about you? How could you?"

"It wasn't as if I had planned it, you know," I replied, feeling my stomach turning. "It wasn't what I wanted, but this is where we are now. Aren't you even a little excited for me?"

Mathieu focused on me as he took my hand. "I am, but this situation is not ideal. I'm sure you can see that, can't you?" he spoke softly, giving my hand a gentle squeeze.

"I want to know when you started working for these people and why?" I said angrily. "This isn't you, what happened to you. Mother would disapprove."

Mathieu shook his head. "This isn't important, Skyler. You need to listen to me." He stood looking around anxiously. "I only wanted to keep you safe, I promise."

Feeling confused and unsure of what he was rambling about, I shook my head and lifted my hands into the air. "Stop, what are you talking about? I am safe. Oh, and by the way, I am also married now." I finished holding out my hand for him to see the beautiful ring.

Mathieu's face fell as I spoke, and he looked at my hand. His mouth dropped open. There was a glimmer in his eyes as he looked into mine. I had seen that look before, but I couldn't place it. "No," he replied as anger flooded his composure. "This wasn't the way it was supposed to be."

He turned away from me, stomping his foot on the ground, clenching his fists. "This is all wrong now," he spat at the air, lifting his head.

"What do you mean?" I asked softly, unable to comprehend what was going on with him. "Mathieu, what is going on, what do you mean?"

As he turned back, I saw his face was red, the veins in his neck stood out as anger seemed to have taken over. The last time I had seen him like this was with our mother's death. The shock of his sudden change made me step back quickly. I felt the bench touching my thigh and sank back down.

"What is happening, Mathieu?" I whispered as dread filled my body. My heart started beating, and I felt hot. "Why do I feel like you did something you shouldn't have?" As the words left my mouth, I picked up movement around us.

Before I could formulate another thought, we were surrounded by the men he worked with. Mathieu gave me a look that spoke of his regret before turning and walking back the way he came.

"Mathieu, Mathieu," I called after him. I tried to run, becoming conscious of the fact that he wasn't going to assist me, but there were too many of them. They captured me, gagged me, and tied my hands before loading me into a car with an elderly man.

"Good day, dear lady," he said in a deep, calm voice as he studied me. "I'm Domique Anchony." he added, waving at the driver to go.

I twisted and turned, trying to get out of the bounds while mumbling into the gag. How could my brother allow this to happen after everything, I wondered. Did he not care about me anymore? Recognizing that there was no way out, I gave up fighting the ties. I crumbled as my shoulders sagged and tears decorated my cheeks.

Mathieu wasn't the man I grew up with. Somewhere something happened that changed him. If I only knew, yet, I felt sure it wouldn't have benefited me in any way even if I knew. An intense feeling of sorrow filled me as we drove inland. Glancing out the window, I saw the ocean getting smaller behind me.

"Don't worry," the man next to me said. "You will not be harmed. Just stay calm and do as you are told." He added, grinning.

His eyes were dark, and so was his complexion. The stench of his perfume, which was applied in overload, stung my nostrils and I wished to smell Luder's fresh ocean aroma. My stomach made a couple of turns as I remembered no one knew where I was going.

Softly, I tapped my head against the window, feeling all hope leave my body. Why did I do such a stupid thing? Why didn't I take Bunny? I trusted my brother. I would never have thought he was capable of such things. He practically raised me and now he was the cause of my heartache. Maybe Luder was right; you couldn't trust anyone.

Everything Luder had told me was true. How long have I been blind, I wondered. I trusted and loved him unconditionally, so much so that I couldn't see anything wrong. We passed the yoga studio going further up. If I could find a way to get out of this predicament, I would find my way there. I was sure Luder would come looking, and he may consider the studio.

A couple of blocks up, the car slowed, and two large steel gates opened. The walls were about two stories high, and the house towered up into the air. Pulling up to the side, I saw the place was swarming with guards. All hope of escaping flew out the door as one of the guards opened to take me out.

Tears were streaming uncontrollably down my cheeks as despair settled in my mind and heart. As the guard carried me inside and stuck me in a room, I could only hope that Luder would eventually find me. I knew he wouldn't give up, but at what cost? This was all Mathieu's doing. I knew how Luder felt, he had just told me. And I would hold onto that to get through.

The room was dark blue, with only a single bed and chair inside. The lights were weak, barely illuminating the room. I tried to sit up on the bed, but the ties around my hands pushed into my wrists. Shifting back, I stopped moving and lay still, hoping the bounds would ease a little.

After all, I thought, staring at the door, Luder promised that nothing would ever happen to me or our child. Thinking of the last time I saw him. I remembered his sullen face. I wished I had stayed and not tried to do things my way. I was sure he would have allowed me to see Mathieu, but it would have been under safer conditions.

Chapter 23 - Luder

After sulking over my cup of coffee, I knew I had to pull myself together. I made a couple of calls following up with the family before sitting on the docks with Bunny. He ran around a bit and settled next to my feet, out of breath.

I took Bunny with me as I left, and I returned to Ivan's club to assist with sorting things out. It relieved me from the stress caused by having her in my life the last couple of days.

Returning, I did feel better, though. I was waiting on the docks as the car pulled in. About time, I thought as I walked towards the car. She had been gone all day.

Even though I was overjoyed with the marriage and the baby on its way, I had some doubts. But once I had time to talk it out with Roman earlier, I felt a hundred percent better. I was ready to do this whole family set-up.

Roman and Sergei had even assisted me in looking at buying a house for us. Grinning at myself, I was ready to welcome her back.

But before I could take the last step, the driver sprang out of the car. "I'm sorry, I'm so very sorry, sir," he rattled out as his feet hit the ground. Glancing up, the guard looked away as he mumbled. "She's gone."

Feeling any and all calmness I had, was replaced by rage, I stormed forward and slammed the driver into the side of the car. "What did you say?" I spat at the guard across the roof, fuming. After everything we've been through, this was the last thing we needed.

"She," the driver started saying.

"Spit it out, Mick," I breathed out.

"We were waiting outside as she had asked." He mumbled.

"You left her alone?" The utter astonishment in my tone was evident.

"She was bringing out her things and I was loading them," the driver added softly as I let go of his throat and stepped back. Then she stopped coming out, so we went in. The front door was open, and she was gone." He finished looking down at the ground.

"Were there any signs of a struggle?" I asked, shoving him sideways to get to the car.

"No, nothing we could see. The place was a mess, but I didn't think it showed signs of a struggle." That was the last I heard as I slammed closed the door and spun out of the gates.

She wouldn't run, would she, I wondered as I raced back to Ivan's club hoping the family was still there. We're married, and she was so excited, I felt sure she wouldn't run.

Pulling into the parking area, I saw the men all outside, getting ready to leave. I was driving so fast. I almost didn't make the stop. I forced my foot down on the brake but also had to pull the handbrake. The car skidded sideways, rumbling up smoke from the tires as it screeched to a halt.

Getting out everyone's attention was on me. "Sorry, Ivan," I said as I paced toward them. "Skyler's been taken," I breathed out. It felt like my heart was about to stop. I had never felt all these emotions now surging through me. I was like a lion tossed into a city zoo.

"Calm down," Ashan said, walking closer and touching my shoulder. "Take some deep breaths and tell us what happened."

Placing my hand on his arm, I heaved as my lungs appeared to be struggling to get air. Ivan also came closer. "You need to calm down, Luder," he said calmly. "We're all here for you, take a deep breath and tell us what happened."

I glanced at him and sucked in as much air as my lungs could keep. Breathing out, I spoke. "She went to her house to get some stuff. I don't know what happened. The guard came back and said she was gone, and the front door was open."

Ivan patted my shoulder. "Okay, just one question, and not because we are judging, just wondering, okay."

I nodded in reply, still breathing slowly to keep myself upright.

"Why didn't you go with her?" His question hit hard as I have been wondering the same thing.

Letting out another deep breath, I looked around. It appeared everyone was wondering the same thing and was waiting for an answer. As a family, we tend to always stick close.

"I don't know," I started. Pushing my hand through my hair, I turned and started pacing up and down. "After everything that had gone down…" Guilt was eating at me, and I couldn't complete what was on my mind. None of the other men would have reacted the way I did.

"Okay," Roman replied, sounding a little too eager. "It's not her fault or yours." He added. "We need to get the family together and first send out the informants to find her whereabouts. We can't simply flood the street with no direction."

"Let's go inside," Ivan said as he turned and headed back in. Ashan nodded his head sideways, and I followed Ivan, with the rest coming back inside as well.

As usual, we gathered in the back room when any form of business needed to be discussed. Seeing as this was serious, Ivan pulled open the corner cabinet and poured each of us a drink.

"I've already spoken to Yuri. He will get Aleksei and Nikolai to help as well. They will scour the city." Sergei spoke up from the back of the room. "Soon, we will have a location."

"Great, now, once we have a location, we can do a quick scan of the place and decide on the best action to take," Ivan noted.

"I know what action is needed," I spoke out loudly. As my words left me, I saw the disapproval on the faces of the men in the room. I was sure most of them had also experienced times when they didn't care about their actions. But I also knew this wasn't how we did things.

"We know you want her back, but don't be stupid, we need to be careful," Roman added. "There was a procedure to follow."

I knew he was right, but my blood was boiling, and my heart was aching. I nodded in acknowledgment and sat down. It didn't take long before we got the call. Having the address, we all took the drive uptown. I rode with Ashan as no one would allow me to drive my own car.

We went in only three cars, and the guards held back until we assessed the situation. Even though it was only a short twenty-minute drive, it felt like it took forever. I could swear they were driving slowly on purpose.

We went up and down the streets surrounding the place. The walls were very high, and the presence of guards was very obvious. This is how we knew we were at the right place. As we passed for the fourth time, the guards started noticing us. Hanging back, we waited for the commotion to quiet down.

Once the guards settled back in their place, we parked down the road to decide the best action plan. We decided to wait for it to get darker before we would execute our plan. Ashan and Roman would drive up and demand to see Domique. They would then ask him what he wanted and what he would like in exchange for Skyler.

While they kept their attention at the front of the house, I would sneak in with the rest and rescue her. At the back, we noticed places where the walls would be accessible. There were also fewer guards at the back. We felt sure the plan was solid. Now, it was a matter of time. While we waited, we grabbed coffee at a corner shop not too far away. I struggled to drink it as my mind kept toiling with all that had passed.

I couldn't help but wonder how they were treating her. Having her around, getting to know her, and being with her has changed me in many ways. I never thought I would ever recover from the pain I suffered in Russia. Yet, here I was, many years later, but more in love than I could have imagined.

I wanted her, no, I needed her. If anything happened to her, I felt sure it would send me over the top. Not even Ashan would be able to control me this time should things go wrong.

"Penny for your thoughts?" I heard Ashan speak next to me.

I hadn't realized that I had been staring at the house without moving for quite some time until he spoke. Coming out of my thoughts, I turned to face him. "Sorry, I was just thinking," I replied.

Ashan grinned and pointed at the huge gates halfway up the block. "Looks like they are changing shifts."

Looking up at the road, I saw the gate wide open as cars pulled in and out. Something was happening, but we couldn't be sure what it was. "What if they decide to move her or move in on one of our places while we just sat here?" I said to Ashan as I picked up the radio. "Guys, maybe we should move, we can't be sure of what is happening?" I spoke out.

"Sure, I think we could move in," Roman replied. Exiting the car, Ashan leaned over the seat, looking up at me. "Be careful, brother," he said.

I nodded and stood watching as he pulled up the road and parked on the street. Soon, Roman's car and two of his guards pulled up as well. They walked to the gate and started talking to the guards.

Sergei pulled in next to me. "You coming?" he asked through the window.

"Just a sec," I replied still looking at the gate. Once I saw Domique joining them, I got in, and we drove around to the back. There were about thirty guards with us as we first walked the back wall. Once we found a spot, we assisted each other up the walls, building a human ladder. Sitting on top of the wall gave a clear view of the backyard and the house.

Only a couple of lights were on, and one of those rooms held my wife. Tired of sitting around waiting, I scanned the wall to both sides. In the furthest corner, the roof of the house was about a meter from the wall.

I tapped Sergei on the arm and pointed to the corner. He nodded in agreement and showed the guards to move that way.

The wall was a double, so I stood up and slowly walked on it to the other side. Sergei only shook his head as I stood up. He climbed back down and joined the guards in the corner. I didn't have time to play it safe, I needed to get into that house.

As I took my last step, he came up the side of the wall. We assisted each other over onto the roof before a couple of the guards joined us. Moving with caution, we headed toward the rooms that had lights on.

The first one was on a lower floor, and we decided to leave that one for now. I hoped she wasn't in there as we would have to go down to the ground to see inside. Moving to the second light, which was a room on the top floor. I lay down on the roof and slowly slid over the side. Leaning over with the men holding my legs I peeked inside.

The room looked like an office, and the door leading to a hallway was open. But she wasn't in there. Shaking my head, they pulled me back up. There were only three more. One was on the very bottom floor, like the first one, and another on the middle floor. The last one on the other side was again on the top floor.

We decided to move to that one next as we would need longer arms to look at the others. Hanging again from the roof, I glanced inside the room. The light wasn't as bright as the other one. The room was filled with shadows as the day started turning into night.

My heart skipped a beat and I almost screamed at them as I saw her. Skyler was lying on the small bed in the dark room, tied and gagged. I felt fury shooting through me seeing her that way. Without thinking, I started swinging myself back and forth trying to grab hold of the small balcony just below me.

I heard whispers from the roof as the men protested my swinging. I told myself there was no other option as I swung harder. I felt the hands around my ankles disappear. Glancing down my body up to the roof, I saw the guys above all standing with worried expressions.

As I realized I was about to drop three stories to the ground, likely killing myself, I felt the cold steel passing my fingers. Closing my hands around the bar, I ended up slamming my body into the wall. Pain shot through me, but the relief was greater. I grinned at the men peeking over the roof, mumbling softly.

I hung from the bottom of the balcony. I didn't make the side, but I did manage to get hold of the balcony.

Feeling my hands slipping as sweat invaded my palms. I started climbing with all the might I had. Gliding onto the balcony, I stood for a second, scanning the room while catching my breath. She was alone, and the door was closed. This was a good sign.

Slowly, I turned the doorknob. But as expected, it was locked. I didn't know why I thought it would be open. I walked to the edge of the balcony. Leaning over the side, I looked up. I made a turning motion with my one hand and then shook my head, hoping they would understand.

They shared some glances, and one of the guards lifted his hand. Soon, they were lowering him halfway down. He handed me two pins. I nodded and then returned to the door as they pulled him back up.

It took me a while as I hadn't done this since my school years. But I did manage to unlock the door. I wiped the sweat from my forehead and put the pins in my pocket.

Softly and slowly, I opened the door and sneaked to bed. Skyler was lying with her back to me. As I came up against the side of the bed, I softly placed one hand on her shoulder and touched her arm as I whispered, "Shhh, it's me, hun."

She flung her head back as far as she could. As her eyes fell on me, they seemed to light up. Even with the gag in her mouth, her smile was clear. I untied her and took the gag out so we could get moving. I didn't want to be caught in here. Skyler threw her arms around my neck, and I moved towards the balcony.

Stepping out on the balcony, we heard voices approaching. Holding her legs, I pushed her into the air so the guards could pull her up. Once she was safely on the roof, I got onto the railing, it was my turn. As the guards pulled me up, I heard the door swinging open. We would need to move quickly, but we had to keep quiet, so they didn't know we were on the roof.

"What," a voice echoed through the room. "It was a distraction," the voice screamed. "Get out there and get them. Use any way necessary."

We realized we didn't have time to be careful. We ran across the roof back to the wall. Skyler went down first, then Sergei and me, before the guards came down. Once on the ground, we flooded into the cars and took off.

Having her in my arms gave me great relief and peace. I held her tight as we drove and never wanted to let go again. Recognizing I had fallen in love, I kissed her cheek and whispered in her ear. "Skyler, you mean so much to me."

She glanced up at me, beaming as she hugged me tighter. We didn't go back to the yacht or Roman's place. I had Sergei drop us off at a hotel for the night. He would collect Bunny and keep him for the night. Tomorrow was another day. We would gather in the morning and make other plans for suitable accommodation.

After booking in under another name we headed upstairs to the penthouse. Skyler clung to me without fail as we moved up and into the room. Once we were alone, we could finally talk.

"I'm so sorry, Luder," Skyler said as the door closed.

I smiled, taking her by the shoulders and holding her in front of me. "No, there is nothing to be sorry about, hun. I am just so happy that you are safe." Grinning, I pulled her back into my arms and just held her. Just having her in my arms gave me peace of mind.

I picked her up and carried her to the chaise. Placing her down, I spoke softly, "You rest, I will pour a bath and order room service. How does that sound?" Skyler smiled and nodded as she rubbed her wrists.

They were quite red with deep lines on them. "Do they hurt a lot?" I asked.

"It's more of a burning than pain," she replied softly.

"In the morning, I will have the doctor take a look, for now, we will clean them and apply some cream. How does that sound?"

Skyler nodded slowly without looking up as she drew a line over the markings with her finger.

Moving to the bathroom, I grabbed the portable landline from its nook. The bath was larger than I thought, but that was perfect. Opening the taps, I poured half a bottle of bubble bath in and dialed room service. The bath was shaped like a large shell, which was fascinating.

Once the bath was more than halfway filled, I closed the taps and lit the candles around the room. Walking out, I glanced back as I turned the light off. It was perfect.

Entering the lounge, the doorbell rang. "Just in time," I said, opening the door. The young man pushed the trolley inside. It was loaded with all kinds of fun foods. "Thanks, you can just leave it here," I said, tipping him.

I pushed the trolley into the bathroom and went back for my bride. Skyler was still on the chaise, looking around the room. She seemed far away as I approached. Tonight, I will make her forget, I swore to myself as I stopped next to her.

Skyler allowed me to pick her up again. I carried her to the bathroom. As we entered, she smiled at me. "This is beautiful," she breathed out softly as I lowered her to her feet.

"Skyler," I said, lifting her head. "I meant what I said. I will always protect you and the baby."

As her lips parted, I leaned in and kissed her. I felt her softly gasping for air as our lips met. She wrapped her arms around my neck. Her mouth was inviting and warm, her kiss was tender.

Slowly, I started removing her clothes. My heart raced as my hands moved over her silky soft skin. In turn, she stripped me of my jacket and shirt. Feeling her tender touch sent trembles up my spine, exploding my brain. This was nothing like before.

Even though we have had sex twice now, this felt different. I felt sweat developing in my palms, removing the last of her clothing. Stepping back to rid myself of my pants, I couldn't help but admire her beauty. She was exquisite, every inch of her gorgeousness making all my senses tingle.

Skyler stood there before me naked, biting her lower lip and swaying lightly from side to side as I tried to get out of the constraints of my pants. My mind went scrambling as my breathing suddenly turned laborious. Stumbling backward as my pant leg caught on one foot, I bounced around, trying not to end up on the floor.

Skyler giggled as I struggled and turned the atmosphere promptly. I stopped, placed my foot down, and stepped on the side of my pants with my other foot. Pulling myself from my pant leg, I stepped up to her and pulled her into my arms.

My skin pricked as our bodies met, and my dick instantly rose to the occasion. I lifted Skyler and lowered her into the tub before pulling the trolley closer and joining her. I poured us each a glass of alcohol-free champagne and pulled her closer.

She was beaming, and I felt satisfied that I was able to lighten her mood. She had been through a lot, and tonight, I wanted her to forget the world outside. Staring at her made my heart leap. My breath caught as she turned and lay back against me, sipping from her glass and caressing my leg.

Adding soap to the sponge, she allowed me to lather her neck, arms, and breasts. As I moved, I felt my dick throbbing against her back. Every inch of my being wanted her. Rinsing her neck and arms, I gracefully placed delicate kisses down her arms.

Skyler turned her head, meeting my lips with pure passion. Her hand reached up and settled in my neck as we kissed. I felt my heart about to burst with love as our lips played and our tongues met.

"I love you," I breathed out into her mouth.

CHAPTER 24 - SKYLER

My wrists burned slightly as I lowered my hands into the water. I knew they would need cleaning and care, but it could wait. Strangely enough, I needed Luder more now than ever before. My body yearned for his touch as he proceeded to wash my neck, arms, and breasts. With each move, my insides turned and twisted, sending vibrations through my body.

His voice was sincere. His words filled me with satisfaction as he whispered while bathing me affectionately in kisses. I wanted him, no, I needed him, he had to help me to forget everything that had happened. I felt sure he would be able to do that.

Placing the glass on the side of the giant tub, I turned to him. On my knees between his legs, I placed my hands on his warm cheeks and looked into his incredible eyes. "Luder," I breathed out slowly. "I love you too."

He grabbed my face and pulled me in, sparks flew as our lips met with force this time. His tongue played with my lips as we kissed, seeking a way inside. Parting my lips, I felt a surge push up my body as he pulled my head sideways, exploring my mouth with his tongue.

Luder gently lifted me onto his lap so I could place my legs around him. Sitting on his lap, I could feel the throbbing between his legs. Heat rose within my pussy as we continued kissing. Holding my hair behind my head, he pulled back and kissed my neck as he came upright in the bath. His breathing was just as labored as mine.

He eased me back, holding my neck in his hand as his kisses moved down my neck to my chest. First, he kissed between my breasts before nibbling tenderly at each nipple, lighting up all my senses. I moaned lightly as his mouth closed over my breast sucking them in while his tongue played with my nipple.

Closing his legs around my middle, I felt him moving. He pushed me back to the side of the tub. We slid until my back was against the side, freeing his hands to explore my body. Looking up at the ceiling, I closed my eyes absorbing every touch. The edge of the tub was surprisingly soft, and I lay comfortably as his hands moved over my shoulders and down my breasts, exploring my body.

I shifted left and then right as his touch ignited my senses. He drew lines from my shoulders over my breasts and down my stomach with his fingers. Trembling under his touch, I licked my lips as my stomach turned with desire.

Luder took hold of my knees and pushed his hands up my legs. As he moved from my knees up, he spread my legs open to the sides. He brought his hands to rest in the arch of my legs next to my vagina. As he moved his thumbs up and down my pussy, I squirmed, feeling the blood rush through my veins. His touch was gentle with just enough pressure.

He placed his thumbs together on the edges of my pussy entrance and slowly pushed them in. I breathed out hard as a moan left my mouth. My muscles pounded as his fingers moved in and out. His touch was hard but exhilarating. My mind was wiped clear of any thought.

My breath caught, and my eyes shot open as he pushed up on my clitoris with his one thumb while penetrating me with his other fingers. I felt him deep inside me. "Oh, baby," I breathed out, glancing at him. As he moved his fingers in and out, I felt the soft pounding turn into an increased pulsing.

Placing my feet next to him in the bath, I slid my bottom up and down as he moved his fingers, stroking all the right spots. My body was moving on its own as I felt my yearning rising with every move. Luder leaden forward, allowing his fingers to find a deeper path as he sucked my nipples.

Shuddering from his touch I grabbed his shoulder as I spoke in a barely audible voice. "Baby, I want you,"

Pulling his fingers out, Luder pressed his pounding dick against me as he pulled me back up. "Not yet, hun," he whispered.

It felt like I was losing my mind. I wanted him inside me, my body craved to be filled with all of him. "Luder," I breathed out heavily, leaving scratches across his back as I pulled him closer.

Placing his finger across my lips, he made a 'shhh' sound before leaning in and kissing me hard. I was exploding; every touch sent chills through me. I was more than ready for him. I closed my eyes and lifted my head as my tongue traveled across my lips. Breathing out slowly, I spoke to him. "I want you,".

Luder placed fond kisses down my neck and over my breasts, making me groan as my pleasure senses lit further. He held my hips firmly in his grip as he pushed me up against the side of the tub. He lifted me until I was seated on the side. Looking down, I saw a glimmer in his eyes as he moved in between my legs.

His hands moved gently up and down my legs. "Relax hun," he whispered sensually as he softly took hold of my knees, pushing my legs to the sides. Feeling the cool wall behind me as I lay back didn't bother me; my body only felt his touch. Luder tenderly licked my pussy lips. His tongue was warm and tender as it moved, shattering my world.

Breathing heavily, I wrapped my fingers around his head as he nibbled my clitoris. My fingers were laced in his soft hair. I couldn't decide if I wanted to open my legs wider or close them around his head as my stomach turned from the pleasure.

He continued to nibble and lick as I clung to his head, growling in different tones. My legs shook with every move he made. I closed them and then opened them. At some point, I lifted them to the sides of the bath and lowered them again as every move shook my being. I shuddered as he pushed his tongue into me, allowing a scream of pleasure to escape my mouth.

Luder pulled back, glancing up at me. "Please take me," I breathed out heaving. He grabbed my hips and pulled me down into the tub onto him. His dick was throbbing excessively as he lowered me onto him.

Feeling his dick penetrate me sent my mind whirling. Grabbing hold of the sides of the tub, I lifted and lowered myself slowly on his big shaft. Luder held my hips tightly as we moved. I knew he was close to coming as his grip tightened.

He pulled my butt forward as I came down again, sending shivers through my clitoris, turning my world upside down. I leaned back, allowing my moans to grow as we moved faster and faster. Luder's dick filled out as he came. My arms, my legs, everything shook as he filled me while I exploded onto him.

Leaning forward I collapsed on his shoulder as our breathing broke into gasps for air. He hugged me tightly while trying to regain his control. Beaming, I kissed his neck.

"I love you so much, Skyler," he whispered kissing my breastbone. "You complete me."

"And you, me," I breathed out.

We sat for a minute just holding onto the moment before he moved back, allowing me to take my place in the tub. We had more champagne, and I ate some of the fruit platters from the trolley.

There was a meat platter, cheeses, and crackers as well. After a couple of bites, Luder pulled me closer and lathered me with soap again, washing my body slowly. I admired the look he held in his eyes, filled with compassion. He washed and stepped out once he had satisfied his need to bathe me.

As I was rising from the tub, he moved in with a towel. Wrapping me in it, he lifted me out and carried me to the bedroom. Laying me down on the soft bed Luder pushed himself up over me. "You are amazing," he spoke before kissing me tenderly.

I beamed at him as I wrapped my hands around his neck, he made me feel loved and safe. "You're not too bad yourself," I replied, grinning.

Our kisses heated up as my hands explored his masculine chest. Trailing his muscles with my fingers, I felt each one tighten as I moved. "My turn," I whispered as he stirred lightly under my touch.

Luder smiled as I pushed him over next to me and sat on top of him. "This could be interesting," he said as I leaned forward and kissed his neck.

"Well, Mr. Morozov," I whispered in his ear. "We have all night, don't we?"

"Yes, that we do, Mrs. Morozov," he replied grinning.

My heart fluttered hearing him say that. I rid myself of the towel to feel his skin against mine. His cock had started stiffening and pounding as I sat back down with nothing between us. Bending forward I left a trail of kisses down his rock-hard abs. He shifted his legs as I moved down and sat on my knees between them.

My arms were stretched up as I moved. Delicately, I dug my nails into his chest, pulling my hands in, I left slight red lines down his body. My kisses continued down to his now pulsing cock. Lifting my eyes toward him, I licked his shaft before speaking in a seductive tone. "I must say, Mr. Morozov, this is more than I expected, twice in one evening. You do have a lot of stamina."

He slightly lifted his head glancing down at me grinning as I stroked his balls. Seeing him faintly shaking made me happy.

I took his dick in my hand, holding it up right slipping the tip into my mouth. Luder lifted his head looking down at me as his breathing started to turn heavy. He tenderly caressed my cheek before laying back down. Playing with my tongue over the tip, I felt his body clenching and relaxing with every move.

After a while, his cock was stiff and pounding. I moved down on it, swallowing as I went, and backed up slowly. Soon he was grabbing at the bed sheets, crumpling them in his hands and pulling tight on both sides.

As he started moaning softly, I moved faster. With every up and down, I also moved my hand, intensifying my grip and releasing with every rub. Soon he was mumbling under his heavy breathing. Quickening my pace, I tasted him like the first time, just as sweet, as he came into my mouth. I wondered if his diet had something to do with the taste.

Holding the tip in my mouth, I moved my hand up and down, allowing him to finish. His legs vibrated next to me as he shook.

Once he was done, Luber leaned down and grabbed hold of my neck. He delicately pulled me up to him. As I was in line with his body, he swung me over onto my back, kissing me with immense passion.

"Thank you," he puffed into my neck, sounding out of breath as he collapsed onto me. After a second or two, I pushed at his shoulders, feeling his pressure crushing my lungs.

"Luder," I said, exhaling out heavily. "You're crushing me, baby."

He got up and sat next to me on the bed, grinning like a cat who had just enjoyed a plate of cream. Turning on my side, I lay against his butt. After a bit, he turned halfway, smiled, slapped my butt, and got up.

"Right," he said walking to the bathroom and glancing back. "I'm just going to take a quick shower and then some coffee."

He disappeared through the door. Laying back I smiled up at the ceiling. Tonight had been amazing, and I wondered if this was what was in store every night. After a while, I got up. Luder had just finished and was drying as I entered the bathroom.

I took a quick shower and dressed in his shirt. Entering the lounge, I found him on the chaise with his coffee. He was dunking rusks into it and taking big bites as he scrambled through the channels on the television.

He looked around as he heard me entering. "I wasn't sure if you wanted something, so I got most of the menu," he said as I moved closer.

Plopping down next to him, he wrapped his arm around me. I pulled my legs up and cuddled in his embrace. Pecking at the platters on the trolley before us. There were some movies, music, and news channels, but none appeared to draw his attention.

Sipping my juice, I waited, considering my options as he searched the stations. I could only hope he would listen to my request without judgment. So much had happened; we would need to talk about things, but I wasn't sure where to start.

I felt him tapping my shoulder. Glancing up, I noticed the television was off. He was staring at me questioningly, pulling his eyebrows together above his nose. "Where did you go just now?" he asked.

Coming back to reality I sat up. "Nowhere, I'm right here," I replied, grinning. "Sorry, I was just thinking," I added as he didn't respond.

"Anything you would like to share, hun?" Luder spoke softly in a kind tone.

"Well," I started glancing around. "I was thinking about Mathieu."

"Your brother," he asked suspiciously. "With everything, you can be thinking of you think of your brother?"

His tone was still soft, so I continued.

Placing both my hands on his chest I leaned in and flickered my eyelids. "I was hoping we could talk about him." Luder's mouth pulled up on one side as I spoke. He took my hands in his and shook his head gradually.

"I'm listening," he said softly, pulling me onto his lap.

Placing my feet next to his sides, I flung my arms around his neck and kissed his cheek. "I know the couple of times you met him wasn't quite friendly." I laid my head down on his chest before continuing.

"He has made many mistakes, and I am sure he regrets everyone. Especially the last one." I added, taking a deep breath.

"Yes, mistakes have been made," Luder replied. "Yet, allowing you to be taken by his boss…" Luder went silent. I could hear his heart beating faster.

Glancing up I saw concern on his face. "That was a choice he made," Luder added softly.

"I know, but that was before he knew we were married," I replied flatly. I still couldn't believe he had done that. But there might not have been another option I told myself. "Would you at least talk to him," I asked, glancing up.

Luder was silent for a bit, surely considering my request. I felt his arms tightening around me before he spoke. "If it will make you happy, hun. But no promises."

Kissing him on the cheek, I added what I actually wanted. "I was hoping there was a way you could maybe assist him in getting out from under his boss." Pulling slightly back from his arms, I waited for his reaction.

"Well," he said. "It isn't only up to me, you know that."

"Yes, but I was hoping you could talk to the family. He could do a lot of good. He's not a bad man."

Luder laughed as he continued. "I could, but I can't make any promises as said. He has been the cause of a lot of trouble."

"I know, I know," I said before leaning in and kissing him hard. "But he had no other option, I'm sure of it."

"Okay," Luder said in a light tone as I got up.

"Thank you," I said, smiling. "I think I'm tired," I added, heading towards the bedroom. "I think I'm going to sleep."

"Sure," Luder replied. "Just finishing my cup, be there in a minute."

Laying down on the soft bed, I could feel sleep calling me. Today had been highly eventful, and I felt drained. As Sleep came, I heard Luder entering. He slipped in behind me and pulled me into a warm embrace.

As my eyes closed and my mind drifted off, I heard him whispering.

"I love you, Skyler."

Chapter 25 - Luder

The sun had barely made its appearance when I woke. Glancing sideways, I saw Skyler still fast asleep. Quietly, I got up, not wanting to disturb her. She needed her sleep with the baby and all she had been through.

She seemed so peaceful, so beautiful and elegant. We may never have gotten to know each other if not for the child. Looking at her, I knew that it would have been catastrophic to never know her love. We were meant to be, I felt sure of it.

Entering the lounge, I opened the blinds and stepped out onto the balcony. The early morning air was cool and refreshing. Leaving the balcony door open, I went back inside and grabbed the phone, calling room service. I ordered a strong pot of coffee and asked them to bring it in without knocking as I didn't want to wake Skyler.

Checking my cell, I saw Ashan had left a message. There was a meeting this afternoon at the club, and they wanted me to bring Skyler. Replying to his text, I wondered what was happening now, but I confirmed that we would be there.

Once the coffee arrived, I checked in on Skyler again before sitting down outside on the balcony. The city was magnificent, but the ocean caught me.

I sat outside on the balcony sipping my coffee and watching the sun rise over the city. In the distance, the ocean lapped at the beach. Today was going to be a calmer day. I could feel it in my bones, the air was clean and fresh.

Once I had my first cup, I checked in on Skyler again. She stirred as I peeked around the door, opening her eyes. "Good morning, hun," I said, walking over and kissing her forehead.

Skyler smiled up at me as she spoke, "Good morning, what time is it?"

"It's still early, rest some more," I replied, walking back to the door. As I left, she turned to her side, closing her eyes again.

I had two more cups before ordering breakfast and tea for her. The sun was up and shining brightly down on us. Once it arrived, I entered the room with the trolley and sat down beside her. "It's time to get up, hun," I said softly, caressing her cheek.

Skyler's eyes flickered a couple of times before she opened them and smiled at me. After stretching, she sat up against the headboard. "Good morning, baby," she uttered, glancing at the trolley. "Is that for me?"

She has been eating more and more with each passing day and her tummy has started growing. It was still small but adorable.

Standing, I replied as I grabbed the bed tray from the bottom and placed it over her legs. "It sure is." Once the bed tray was standing solidly, I placed her plate and cup of tea on it.

Sitting on the bottom of the bed, I pulled the trolley to me so I could get to my plate. After breakfast, she had a quick shower while I ran down and bought her some clothing from the store next to the hotel. Not sure about her size, I grabbed a couple of outfits in different sizes.

Except for her size, I didn't even know what she preferred. But thinking of the clothing I had seen her in, I was sure she would like some of the ones I got her.

Entering the suite, she was waiting on the chaise with no clothing on and a wide smile. "Oh, my," I said, closing the door behind me. Checking my watch, I realized we didn't have much time. I allowed her to sleep as late as possible. Seeing her there, I regretted that decision, but it was done.

I placed the clothes down beside her as I leaned in and kissed her. "I'm sorry, hun," I whispered. "We have to get going, or we going to be late."

Skyler opened the back and started fumbling through the clothing as she eyed me. "Late going where?" she questioned.

"A meeting with the family," I uttered, collecting my keys, and phone. I checked and made sure there wasn't anything else I needed to take.

"Have you asked?" she said, pulling on a bright yellow dress and lacy black underwear.

"No, but they let us know there is a meeting, and we're running late," I added, tapping her butt as we moved to the door. "You are sexy," I said. I hadn't booked out yet as we still needed to decide where we were going. I locked the suite door and put the keys in my pocket.

The car was waiting for us as we exited the lobby. There was no immediate sign of trouble and I hoped we wouldn't have any issues today. Driving to Ivan's club went without hassle. I pulled around to the side and parked with the rest of the family.

Everyone seemed to have gone inside. I knew we were the last to arrive as I noticed Ashan's car parked just a couple of spaces from mine. He has always been the last to meetings. However, that seemed to have changed. Grinning at myself, I took Skyler's hand and headed inside.

The place was dark and quiet as we walked through the side door. I wondered if everyone was in the small back office. Yet, I felt sure all the men and women wouldn't fit. As we moved through the place, I checked the kitchen and even the storage room, but the place appeared deserted.

This made me uncomfortable as I had never seen the place so empty. So much had happened in the last couple of weeks, and this wasn't normal. I pulled Skyler in behind me as we moved down the narrow passage.

"What's wrong," she questioned, lowering her voice and holding my shoulder.

"I'm not sure," I replied pulling my gun from under my jacket. I was glad I had strapped it on before we left. I kept it in the car most of the time as I didn't feel it was always essential. Yet, with the days we have had, it was always needed it seemed.

The office door was slightly ajar, but it was also dark. Even though it was past ten in the morning, darkness filled the club. Ivan had it painted black to enhance the neon effect with parties. Yet, it made the club very dark, even during the day if the lights were off.

Stopping before the office door, I nudged it with the tip of my gun. It creaked as it slowly opened. There was no movement or sound from within. My heart rate picked up as I stepped forward to flip the light switch. As I touched the switch, I felt a lump forming in my throat.

What was happening, where was everyone? The cars were all parked as usual outside. Something terrible has happened, my mind yelled.

Skyler clung to my jacket as the light came on. The room was empty. There was no one inside. Hearing movement behind us, I swung around, pulling Skyler with me so she could stay behind me. My gun was lifted and ready to fire.

But the hall was bare. What kind of dream was this? Everyone couldn't be gone, it was impossible. With care, I moved back to the club floor. Skyler now clutching my arm tightly.

Glancing at her, I saw the fear in her eyes. "It's okay," I whispered, moving little by little. Exiting the hall, I stopped and studied the dark room, listening for movement. Everything appeared quiet. Even the wind outside was still.

Pulling my phone from my pocket, I dialed Ashan's number. As the phone rang, I saw its light come on across the room. Dropping my phone to the floor, I held my gun with both hands as I briskly walked across the floor toward it.

My brother's phone was on the table at the back, but the place was empty. This didn't feel right, something was off. Sweat broke out on my forehead as I turned in circles, calling Ashan's name. Skyler stood against the wall where we had exited the passage. Both her hands over her mouth as if holding in a scream.

I felt my mind swirling as my thoughts traveled through every move at the speed of light. Before I could decide what to do next the main doors of the club flew open behind me, the lights went on and the family streamed in from outside.

Ashan came up to me laughing, holding out his hands to hug me. "What the hell, Ashan," I spat at him, shoving him back from me.

"Aaaa, come on, brother, it was funny watching the two of you going crazy in here," he replied amused.

I walked briskly to Skyler and placed an arm around her. "This was not funny guys," I repeated as they gathered before us. "With everything that has happened, this wasn't funny."

"You wanted to be late," Roman said from the back. "Come on, we have a surprise for the two of you," Roman said up, stepping forward.

"Well, this surprise sucked," I added, glancing at Skyler. She was relieved but I could see it had an impact on her. "Are you okay?" I asked, kissing her cheek. "I'm sorry, excuse my family."

Skyler nodded as Ashan brought a chair for her. She sat down and took the glass of water Sam held out to her. Ivan and Sergei joined Roman and Ashan before us as the rest formed a semi-circle around them.

"We have come up with three options," Roman started. "Seeing that the three of us have extra properties," he added, pointing to Ivan, Sergei, and himself.

"They have decided you can have your pick of a home," Ashan spat out, unable to control his excitement as he bounced in one place.

The three of them each handed us a folder containing all the details and images of their extra houses. I was shocked by all of this turmoil for a place to stay.

"We can't, thank you, but we will get a place," I said, holding out the folders for them to take back.

"Nonsense," Ivan responded, pushing the folders back. "We're a family, man."

Glancing down, I saw the curiosity in Skyler's eyes. Handing her the folders, I look back at the cousins. "Can we talk, guys?" I asked.

They looked at each other and nodded. We walked to the office, and I closed the door behind us. I wasn't sure how to start, but I knew this had to be done. The quicker we could decide the better.

"This must be important," Ivan noted as they stopped in front of the table and turned to me.

Clearing my throat, I spoke, "I know we have had a lot of trouble since the day I kidnapped Skyler." The three nodded in agreement.

"Well, I wouldn't call it trouble," Ashan added, grinning.

"Okay, okay, a lot of conflict and problems. But I think we can put an end to it peacefully."

Roman rubbed his chin and Ivan only shrugged. "Continue," Sergei added, giving Ashan a warning look.

"Just hear me out before you give your opinion. Consider my suggestion before making a decision." I uttered wiping the back of my neck. "Skyler asked if we could consider offering her brother a spot here, with us."

Roman and Ivan flinched as my words filled the room. Ashan's mouth hung open but Sergei showed no reaction.

"I know he has made life almost unbearable. But if he was on our side, we could use his knowledge to take down Domique once and for all."

I saw a light in Roman's eyes and knew he saw the possibilities. "We would have to talk about it," he said, looking at Ivan. "Maybe you can give us some time," he finished as he walked past me and opened the door.

"One thing at a time," Ivan added, coming closer. "Let's first go see if your wife has chosen a house."

My mood was lighter as we joined the rest of the family back in the club. Karine, Irina, and Sam were sitting with Skyler as we returned. They were having tea and laughing. Even though we are married, Skyler still throws me off guard with her brilliant smile.

"She's made her mind up, guys," Karine said as we approached them. Roman put his hand around her middle and pulled her into his arm.

"Made up her mind about what?" I asked as I sat down next to Skyler, placing my hand on her leg.

Beaming, she held out one of the files. Taking it and placing it down before me, I glanced around at everyone gathered around the table. All eyes were on me. Opening the folder, I saw it was Roman's second house.

"It's perfect for you both," Karine exclaimed. It's got a private dock for your yacht. A view of the ocean and enough space for little ones." She was almost more ecstatic than Skyler, who was beaming at me now.

"Thank you, really, but we can't," I insisted, closing the folder and moving it to the others on the table.

"There's no such thing," Roman added as he hugged Karine. "We insist."

"Well, with that settled," Ivan spoke up. "We will have the guards sent, and the woman can assist Skyler in getting settled. There is business to discuss."

Looking at Skyler she was still shining brightly. I couldn't break her mood, so I just nodded. She kissed my cheek and left with the women of the family. I still strongly wanted to protest but accepted the gift for now. Later we would find and settle in our own place.

We gathered at the bar counter as Ivan poured us a drink. "Ashan will assist you with setting up the security at the house and if there is anything, just let us know," Roman said, tapping me on the back as he sat down beside me.

"Thanks again," I said. But before I could add anything else, I was silenced by Ivan.

"Back to the topic at hand," he said with authority and clearness in his voice drawing everyone's attention. "If we decide to give Mathieu a chance, it will only be because of family. He has been a thorn in our sides, and he can thank his sister for the opportunity."

Everyone nodded in agreement. Clearing my throat to speak up, Ivan held up a finger, so I waited.

"It will be in a position at the bottom, far away from any actual detail on any of our operations," Ivan added.

"Agreed," the men replied in one voice.

"Right," Sergei said, speaking up. "The other matter you asked about," he continued, looking at me. "We have found a place. It's been vetted, and restorations are on the way. Later, we can sit down, and I can show you the plans, layout, and progress."

"Thanks," I said, nodding. "You are all truly the best."

"There are two warehouses with stock that require care. I think we should visit both and assess the situation." Roman added to the discussion. "The buyers will be in town next week."

"Yes, we can go do that now," Ivan stated placing down his glass. We left the club all in good spirits, even with all that had been going on.

I rode with Ashan as we left. I knew Skyler was safe now and could get back to tending to business. We needed to get the shipments moving again. This deal was vital and to ensure things went as planned we had scheduled the meet for the early morning hours.

These clients have been with us for many years, and they did not take kindly to problems. I hoped we could get this Domique war settled before they came through. Once the crates were counted, the wares checked, and double-checked, we knew things were ready.

Heading back to the club, we had another couple of drinks, making sure our schedules met before each went their way.

I was excited to get home and share the news with Skyler. I could only hope her brother wouldn't pull another stunt on us. The family was going out of their way for him. It made me a bit uneasy as I still felt he was a loyal soldier and might stick it out with Domique.

But you never knew what the future held, and he may end up surprising me. For Skyler's sake, I hoped he would walk straight.

CHAPTER 26 - SKYLER

The pictures they showed me surely didn't do the house justice, I thought as we drove through the big steel gates and up the driveway. The place was surrounded by guards inside and out, it seemed. Karine pulled up and parked in front of the first garage door. There were three, and there was enough space for about ten vehicles if you asked me.

Stepping out of the car, I looked up in awe at the white double-story house before me. Every room appeared to have large wooden windows. Toward the side and the back of the garages, I could see the bright green lawn running around. There were trees and flower beds, and it stretched out far.

Turning to our left, was a thin pathway running around the side of the house to the back. It looked like it led you to a forest as the ground around it was covered in grass, flowers displaying all the colors of the rainbow, and giant trees. The trees formed a canopy over the pathway, which was glorious to see. Karine walked out ahead with the keys.

The front door sat almost at the corner of the house. The front area wasn't as elegant as Roman and Karine's house, but the pure beauty of the place was more than I expected. Following Karine, we stepped through the front door into a dream.

The inside was also white, but everything appeared to be sparkling. The pure whiteness of the place was almost blinding. Around the middle of the wall was a thin gold stripe running right around. There was a small gold-colored table by the entrance door. Plus, there were two more doors leading further into the house.

From the smile on Karine's face, I knew she could see the amazement on my face as I tried to take in everything. Walking to the door on the left, Karine spoke as she pushed it open.

"This door leads to the kitchen, dining hall, lounge, and back yard." Walking to the door on the right, she opened it as she continued. "This door leads upstairs to the three rooms, library, study, and office. There is also an entertainment room."

Grinning widely, I skipped to the left, entering the open-plan kitchen, dining hall, and lounge. The rooms were huge and covered the entire bottom floor. To my right, the kitchen looked like it was suited for a restaurant. It was fitted with an in-house BBQ, eye-level oven, stove, dishwasher, fridge, freezer and so much more.

On the left lay the dining hall with a long table and seating able to seat the entire family. Against the back wall were what looked like hot trays and a serving station.

Walking forward into the lounge and towards the glass doors leading to the back, I felt like a princess. I twirled in circles with my hands up in the air. Karine, Sam, and Irina all stood smiling in the doorway. I had never before seen such beauty, never mind living in it. My heart fluttered with delight.

The living area had a bar, a wall-sized television, and a variety of different chairs and couches.

We explored the second floor, visiting each room as Irina and Sam made us some tea. Karine assured me they would arrange for all our stuff to be moved here over the next few days. Once I had seen the entire house, we joined the other two back in the kitchen.

"You want to sit outside?" Karine asked, picking up her cup.

Nodding enthusiastically, she led the way out to the backyard. The visiting area had a BBQ built in, a bar, and what looked like a serving area with ten tables and chairs. In the corner between the fields of grass was a swimming pool. The yard itself was green, with trees and flowers all around.

We visited outside for more than an hour, chatting about babies, the men, the family, and more. Afterward, the three of them left, and I could start to settle. Soon enough, Sergei had his guards bring Bunny and my belongings from the yacht.

Bunny was just as excited as I was to be there. He ran in and out, from room to room, and sniffed the place up before settling on the dog bed outside. After exploring the house once again, I decided to take a swim before starting supper. I didn't even know if there was food, but if there wasn't, Luder could always order in. He was good at that, I thought walking to the pool.

I had just gotten into the pool when I heard rustling in the bushes. Bunny's ears lifted, but he didn't growl, so I felt no need to call for help. I swam a couple of lengths and then sat on the side next to Bunny.

Bunny jumped up and ran to the bushed. "Bunny," I called. "Bunny, come back boy." I knew the place was closed properly and he couldn't get out. But who knew what was in those thick bushes?

Rising, I wrapped a towel around me before strolling over to where Bunny had entered the brush. Standing there, I called out to him. "Bunny, here Bunny, come boy."

Bunny came bouncing out almost knocking me over. "Slow down boy," I uttered pushing him away from me. Looking up I almost screamed with surprise as I saw him. There in the brush stood Mathieu.

"Come, Bunny," I said, turning to go back in.

"Wait," Mathieu said softly as he took hold of my arm. "Please, I am sorry."

Swinging around, I looked sternly at him, brushing off his hand. "Just one scream and the guards will surround you," I uttered, feeling my stomach churning. "Get away, I don't want to talk to you."

"Please, Skyler, please, hear me out," Mathieu said, lifting his hands up to the sides of him and shrugging. "Just give me a couple of minutes before you have me shot."

His face and eyes portrayed his sorrow, and I couldn't help but feel sorry for him. "You got yourself into a lot of trouble, and then you had me kidnapped," I added, stomping my foot.

"I know, I know, but hear me out, please," Mathieu begged.

Glancing around, I knew we couldn't move back to the house as the guards would see him. "Fine, you have two minutes," I replied, sitting down on the lawn.

"Sis, you're making a big mistake marrying Luder. Both you and the child's life will be in constant danger." Mathieu started.

I lifted my hand out before me showing him to stop. "You have no right, are you saying we would be safe with you? No, look what you got us into."

"Yes, I know, this is all my fault, and I am sorry. But…" I cut him off before he could speak further.

"No, no butts. You have made your choice and so have I." Taking a deep breath, I made sure there were no guards in sight.

"These people, you don't know them and what they are capable of." Mathieu blabbered on.

"And you do?" I asked, raising my voice.

"I just want to keep you safe," he added as I stood up.

"It's too late, we're married. But I have spoken to them, and Luder wants to meet you. He can help you with a position with them." I added softly.

"Skyler," Mathieu responded, his voice rising. "No, you have no idea what you've done." He grabbed hold of his head and turned in a circle on his heels.

"Mathieu, just meet him and hear him out. We can be together as we were when we were younger." I added reaching out.

Mathieu stepped closer and took hold of my shoulders. "Skyler," He glanced around nervously. "Think of your child."

"I am," I responded, stepping back. "Luder is the father, and you know as well as I do that a child needs both parents. Plus, he is a good man."

Mathieu laughed as he walked backward away from me. "Let me know when and where, and I'll be there," he said before disappearing into the brush again.

Bunny ran into the brush barking but didn't stay away long. Walking back to the house I wondered how Mathieu had gotten in. Maybe this place wasn't as safe as I thought. After all, if he could get in and out without being seen, who knows who else could do that?

I was just glad he came alone this time. Entering the house, I decided to talk to Luder about it. We would have to secure that spot and ensure there are no other unsecured places. Especially knowing the business he is in, I felt sure Domique wasn't the first and wouldn't be the last.

I checked the kitchen cupboards and the fridges trying to decide what to make for supper. There weren't a lot of things to choose from, so I decided to go shopping instead of waiting for Luder.

Not sure what time Luder would be home. I didn't want to go too far. The driver took me to the closest store. I got a variety of meats, fruits, some dry goods, tinned goods, and snacks. Suddenly, I had a craving for ice cream, so I bought a couple of tubs as well.

Once back home, I had ice cream for lunch while unpacking before starting supper. Hopefully, in a week or two, I can return to assisting at the shelter and have some stability I thought as I hung my clothing. Holding my favorite pants up, I knew I would have to get other clothes as well soon.

Luder came home sooner than I expected, but the food was cooked. I was in the library when he arrived searching for a good book to read. After I helped him put away his things, we sat outside having tea and coffee before supper.

"I saw Mathieu today," I said casually, sipping some tea and studying his face.

Luder stood quickly from his chair. "Where did he come in?" he asked. "What did he want?"

"The guards should look at the walls covered by brush, especially down by the pool," I responded calmly.

Luder called one of the men and instructed them for new perimeter walks. Turning back to me, he nodded as he spoke. "So, does he want to meet?"

Smiling up at him, I nodded. "Yes, he said we must let him know when and where."

Luder walked over and kissed my cheek. "Let me make some calls. I do hope this isn't one of his traps though," he said, walking in.

After my tea, I headed to the kitchen and dished up supper. Luder returned just in time as I placed the plates down. "Ready for supper?" I inquired.

He smiled at me, and we sat down. Once we were done, we rinsed the plates, cutlery, and glasses before putting them in the washer. It was our first night in this house, and I noticed the tub was about as large as the one at the hotel.

Walking upstairs Luder told me to let Mathieu know he would be meeting him in the morning. They have agreed to offer him a place in the ranks. The meeting was to take place at one of the family establishments down on the beach.

While Luder filled the tub, I made the call. This time, we exchanged roles. I took the lead in the tub and Luder when we went to bed.

Staring up at the ceiling out of breath, I felt sure it could be a boy. My hormones were too uneven for it to be a girl. Also, I generally felt calmer and more sensual than ever before. I had heard women discussing such things but have never considered the implications.

Luder drove me wild just entering a room. Glancing at him, my chest filled with a warm glow. Tomorrow, he would sit down with Mathieu and with him joining the family, I could sleep easier. I rolled over and cuddled in his arms as we fell asleep.

CHAPTER 27 - LUDER

Standing at the door watching Ashan leave, I decide to make Skyler breakfast and surprise her while it's still early. After chopping the fruit and adding them to the bowl, I added some cream just as I'd seen her make it on the yacht.

I hadn't really seen her eat anything else this early, so this had to be her go-to meal. Bunny scratched at the glass door. Walking over to open it, I gently reprimand him. "The door has been open, why didn't you go out then? Now you scratch at my glass door. Naughty boy."

Bunny bounced out even before I had the door open far enough. As soon as his head fit through, he forced himself out. He really needed to get out, I thought walking back to the kitchen counter.

Placing the bowl on a tray, I poured her some tea and added a glass of juice, just in case. Carefully, I took it upstairs and pushed the bedroom door open with my foot. Skyler was sitting up with Bunny turning in circles next to her.

"Hey," I protested. "When did you come back? I swore he was just outside. Get off the bed Bunny."

Skyler laughed as he sat up and looked at me, turning his head from side to side.

"Breakfast in bed," she said as I placed the tray down beside her. "You know a lady can get used to such things. What's the occasion?"

Kissing her, I replied. "No occasion, except for you being here. Plus, I was up so I thought I would surprise you."

"Thank you," she replied, picking up the glass of juice. "This is nice, and you already know what I like."

Grinning, L left her to eat. I took a quick shower and got ready for the meeting. "What are your plans for today?" I asked, entering the room again to get a tie.

"I'm not sure. Maybe I'll go to Irina's spa, she invited me to come any time. But I'll call first." Skyler replied between bites of fruit salad.

"That sounds nice. I shouldn't be too long, though, if you want to do something later." I said, kissing her forehead and heading to the door.

"It sounds good, see you later then." I heard her add as I walked down the stairs.

Before leaving, I made sure the guards would keep an eye on the walls and double their shifts.

Arriving at the restaurant, I noticed there were a couple of regulars and quite a few vehicles parked outside. Some still had people sitting in them. I wondered if these were about to leave or had just arrived. Ashan was standing at the door as I approached.

"Morning, is he here yet?" I asked glancing at the people at the tables.

"Nope, but I have a bad feeling about this." He replied, chewing a piece of gum.

Roman, Sergei, and some of the others were already having coffee at the table in the back corner as we joined them. The waitress had just brought us our cups when Mathieu walked in through the door. He stood and scanned the room, nodding to two men seated closer to the door.

"He's not alone," Roman uttered, rising from the table. We expected as much. Mathieu wasn't here to talk.

Taking a sip of coffee, I also stood up and waved at Mathieu, signaling him to come to us. Roman informed the guards to stand ready as we expected trouble.

"Hi," Mathieu said, extending his hand in a greeting.

Stepping forward, I reached out and shook his hand as I spoke. "Morning, no hard feelings I take it."

Mathieu glanced over his shoulder. "None from me and you?" he added looking back at me.

"This is Roman, Sergei, and Ashan," I said, pointing to each, not bothering to answer him on that as I did still feel offended. "Take a seat, let's talk," I added as I sat back down in my seat.

Mathieu pulled out the chair next to Ashan and sat down. The darkness of the corner thickened with the stiffness in the air. Roman waved at the waiter for more coffee before taking his seat.

I could see on everyone's faces that they were ready for anything. Once Mathieu had his coffee, I cleared my throat before speaking. "So, we have talked about it and are prepared to offer you a place within our ranks."

Mathieu glared at me, lifted his cup, took a sip, and slammed it down. There was a sudden change in his posture as the cup hit the table. Rising, he spat at me from across the table. "You had no right to marry my sister and keep her from me."

"What is wrong with you? We are here because of her, if not for her, you would've been dead already." I inquired as I rose. All the men were standing around the table now.

Mathieu stepped back as the doors swung open and Domique entered. As we expected, he told his boss about the meeting. We would have to end this today, one way or another. At least, this time, we were prepared. Our men were present and informed.

"This is a private meeting Domique, you weren't invited," Roman called across the floor.

Laughing, he replied with a certainty in his voice I didn't like. "Oh, but I was invited. Mathieu works for me, and a meeting with him is one with me."

Glancing at Roman, I knew we would be acting soon. I stepped around the table towards Mathieu. "Look," I stated, looking him in the eye. "We're offering you this because Skyler asked, so either take it or leave as we won't be offering it to you again."

Mathieu grinned at me as he pulled his gun from the side holster. This wasn't needed, but it was happening. Ashan and I bounced around the table as Sergei shoved it over. Bullets came flying towards us but we both made it behind the upturned table in time. Everyone knew not to shoot Mathieu unless it was your life or his.

Turning, we returned fire. Mathieu had also ducked behind a table closer to the door. This was good as we could try and miss him. We could hear the guards outside screaming at each other and doing their part. Inside, we were about to destroy the restaurant.

My heart sank knowing this was the third place since all of this started. I knew the family didn't blame Skyler or me, yet I felt responsible. But knowing her brother was behind all of this must be eating her, and I wanted another outcome here today, for her.

A sharp sulfur smell filled the room with notes of ammonia. Glancing around the side of the table, I aimed at Domique, who had moved to Mathieu. I tried to not hit Skyler's brother as that would not be suitable.

With the amount of noise, I felt sure we would have some other company soon, and this had to end quickly. Rising from my perch I took a couple of shots in different directions. Some of their men lay bleeding close to the door while some of our guards sat against tables and others lay at the doors.

It was a blood bath and couldn't continue much longer as men fell around us. As I pulled the trigger, feeling the recoil of each shot, I could see Skyler in my mind's eye. I tapped Ashan on the shoulder; he knew what the signal was for.

As he rose, we stepped around the table, each pulling our second gun out. We lay down fire as we moved forward. The two-handed brothers. Glancing sideways, I noticed Roman and Sergei had also joined in. The four of us formed a line and shot bullet after bullet as we advanced on Domique and Mathieu.

Some of our guards had also cleared the front and entered through the door. There was nowhere to run, we had them cornered. Men were screaming around us as blood filled the air. The bodies fell left and right. We had to step over some as we moved.

A coppery smell combined with the ammonia hanging in the air. I felt it tickle my nostrils. The sneeze crept up and I knew it couldn't be stopped. I felt a bullet grazing my arm as Ashan went down next to me.

Turning, I saw one of Domique's men advancing from the side. Swinging my one hand out I shot straight between his eyes. No one shoots my brother and lives. Feeling the rush increasing, I turn my full attention to Domique. I turned just in time to see him rise aiming at Roman.

Judging the distance and men between us, I flung myself forward, squeezing both triggers. His body moved left and right as our bullets decorated his chest. Both Roman and Sergei had also seen his move. Yet, it was his last. As he breathed out his last breath going down next to Mathieu, I saw reality entering his eyes.

Mathieu rose, dropped his gun, and screamed out at the top of his voice. "Stop, stop, I give up."

Roman raised his hand, and the guards stopped. There were only a couple of Domique's men still standing, they also dropped their guns and raised their hands.

Holstering my guns, I ran to Ashan's side. "Brother," I breathed out as I lifted his upper body. "Are you okay?"

Ashan smiled as he coughed. "I'm fine," he managed to say before passing out. Sergei made two calls and soon Ashan was on his way to the private hospital we frequented.

Ivan and some of the other family arrived shortly. They got there even before the ambulance to assist with the clean-up. The bullet hit Ashan in the shoulder, but Ivan was positive he would be fine.

The guards dragged the dead out back leaving trails of blood across the floor. Those with minor injuries were treated by the ladies as they arrived, and the others were sent to hospital.

Mathieu sat quietly at one of the tables as we cleared the place out. Roman nodded at me to try again. Mathieu looked up as I walked over. "Have you had enough?" I asked angrily.

"This is not what I expected," he replied sullenly.

"Well, then. Come with me and you can see your sister, let's chat about the future, okay?" I didn't want him near me or her, but I knew I had to accept it. At least the real threat was out of the way.

Mathieu nodded and followed as I left the restaurant. He rode with me to the hospital where they had taken Ashan. I called Skyler and asked her to meet me there. As we drove, I offered Mathieu another chance to join us.

This time he accepted without question. "I'm sorry about your brother," he added looking out the window.

"I would say I was sorry about Domique, but I would be lying," I replied feeling my anger calming down. "If it wasn't for Skyler, you would be dead as well, I hope you know what that means."

155

Mathieu nodded but said nothing more. The rest of the way to the hospital was quiet. Upon our arrival there, we found Skyler waiting. Pulling her into my arms I felt her calmness fill me. Her embrace was warm and soothing.

After holding her tight for a few seconds, I kissed her and then went to find the doctor. She waited with Mathieu in the waiting room. I was sure they had some matters to discuss, especially after the turn of today.

Ashan was in surgery, and I would have to wait for the doctor to finish before they could give me an update. The nurse did, however, add he was stable as they pushed him in. This was good news. Feeling a bit more at ease, I grabbed coffee and headed back to Skyler.

Skyler and Mathieu were sitting in the back corner as I returned. I could see they were deep in a heated discussion. I stopped at the door and waited until Skyler noticed me. She rose and briskly walked to me.

"I'm so sorry for all the trouble he's caused, Luder," she said softly as I handed her a cup.

Mathieu didn't join us at the door, he sat waiting. Leaning in, I kissed Skyler's cheek before speaking. "It's not your fault hun, please don't blame yourself."

The smile she gave me as we moved was gloomy and my heart ached for her. I knew she felt responsible, and it wouldn't change her mind no matter what I said. We sat down with Mathieu as it would still be a while before we knew Ashan's state.

We sipped our cappuccinos in silence, each of us within our minds. It was almost an hour before the doctor appeared at the door. I rose and quickly paced to meet him halfway across the floor. Skyler held my hand as he spoke.

"Mr. Morozov?" he inquired, looking at me.

"Yes," I replied hastily.

"Your brother was lucky; the bullet missed any vital arteries. With enough rest, he will recover fully."

I breathed out loudly as I shook the doctor's hand. "Thank you so much."

"He will need to rest, please make sure of that. At least about two months," he added, pulling his hand from mine.

"Right," I replied, grinning. "May I see him?"

"Sure, the nurse will show you where he is," the doctor said waving at one of the nurses.

Skyler and Mathieu followed to Ashan's room but waited outside for me. Ashan was still very drowsy as I took his hand. "Hey brother, the doctor said you're going to be fine. You just need to rest, okay."

Ashan gave me a weak smile as he slowly opened his eyes. "Yeah, sure thing." He spoke softly and his voice was raspy.

Knowing he was going to be good eased my heart and mind. I sat with him for a bit until Roman and Karine arrived. The family would all be around during the afternoon.

"I'm heading home," I whispered to Roman as they entered his room. "I'll be back later again." He shook his head in acknowledgment and tapped my shoulder as I left. "He will not be alone," he added.

"Let's go home," I said, taking Skyler's hand and heading to the exit. Outside, we tried to decide where Mathieu would go. He couldn't return to his home as some of Domique's gang may show up. We needed to wait for the heat to die down first.

We agreed that he could stay with us for now until we sorted everything out. I had the yacht parked at the new dock, and he could use that in the meantime. With that settled, we headed home.

After supper, I went back to the hospital to sit with Ashan for a bit. He was already feeling better. After an hour of his weak jokes, I had to leave. Too much time with him would drive anyone insane.

I was relieved that he was back to being himself and could now focus on the situation at home. On my way home, Roman called with good news. Excited, I couldn't wait to get home.

Chapter 28 - Skyler

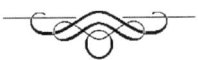

After Luder left for the hospital, I rinsed the evening's dishes and packed the washer. Mathieu stayed for a last cup before heading out to the yacht. We had a good conversation after Luder left and made peace with almost everything.

Even though I was relieved that nobody got seriously injured. At least no one within our family. I had noticed a dull ache developing in my stomach during the afternoon. After supper, I also felt nauseated, which could all simply be due to the stress combined with my pregnancy.

At first, I brushed it off as nerves with everything that had happened. But now that things were calmer it worried me a bit. I headed upstairs and took a warm bath trying to soothe the pain and ease my body.

As I stepped out of the bath, I heard Luder returning from his visit. Pulling my robe on, I walked down to greet him. As I took the last three steps, Luder picked me up and swung me around.

"I have good news," he proclaimed as we turned and turned.

Laughing, I felt my nerves settling. "Stop, stop," I said. "You're going to make me sick."

He was in a very good mood. Without lowering me, we walked to the lounge, and I wrapped my legs around him. He stopped at the chaise and carefully lowered me down. Leaning over me, holding himself up on the sides, he beamed down at me.

"Okay, okay," I said laughing. "What has gotten into you suddenly?"

"Soon, hunny. You only have to wait a couple of weeks, but very soon, hun," he replied cheerfully before leaning in. Luder's kiss was hard but filled with passion.

My stomach twisted and turned as his tongue found its way in through my lips. My hormones were very unpredictable, and I felt an increasing need for him. As his kisses moved down my neck, my hands undid the buttons of his shirt.

I was about halfway with them when he pulled up and yanked his shirt off. The remaining buttons went flying through the air. Coming back in, his chest muscles bulged. Licking my lips as desire filled my veins, I reached up and caressed his chest.

Luder breathed in deeply, lifting his face to the ceiling. I felt a rush filling my body as his next move sent my mind flying. Luder brought his legs in, shoving mine open as he picked me up, turned, and sat down with me. He ripped open the robe and kissed my breasts with force.

I couldn't help but moan as pleasure traveled through my body. Luder grabbed hold of my hips and pulled me into him. I could feel the bulge in his pants. A surge of electricity ran through me as my lust rose even more. He swung me back around as I fumbled with the button of his pants.

But before we could attempt anything, we heard a noise coming from the door to the back patio. Luder sat up and glanced at the door. He swiftly grabbed his shirt from the floor and covered my bosom before getting up. I was fully naked and lying on part of the robe.

His shirt was barely enough to cover my breast. I wondered what he was thinking. Peeking over the side of the chaise, I saw Mathieu standing in the doorway. Luder glanced at me and rolled his eyes, making me giggle. Sitting up I held his shirt to me as I tried to gather the sides of the robe, glad that the back of the chaise was so high.

"Is everything alright?" I asked, wishing he would just go away. I wanted to continue with Luder, but his timing was the worst. Having him here may not have been the best decision.

"Sorry, I was just wondering what time I should be in?" Mathieu uttered as he stared at the floor. "Plus, I saw the light on and was hoping to talk to Luder and get a cup of coffee."

Growling under my breath I rose and went upstairs. "Why had I insisted he stay with us?" I questioned the bedroom walls changing into nighties. My desires ran wild. Dressing was difficult while trying to calm my mind as well. I didn't want coffee or tea, I wanted Luder, and Mathieu was turning the evening into work.

Pulling up my pants, I stomped the floor. I should have locked the door when he left earlier. So, it's partially my fault as well. But how was I supposed to know he would return this time of the evening?

Once I was dressed more appropriately, I returned downstairs to make some coffee. "One cup," I mumbled, entering the kitchen. The two men were standing on the patio, deep in discussion and didn't even hear me.

Placing the cups on the lounge table, I called out. "Luder, Mathieu, the coffee is ready."

Inside, I was boiling, and it wasn't easy to control my emotions. I paced up and down the kitchen, waiting for them to conclude their talks so we could turn in for the evening. This time, I was making sure the doors were locked. We would not be disturbed again.

After a while, they entered and sat down. Luder seemed at ease being half-dressed before Mathieu. It didn't appear to fade Mathieu either. I supposed men were used to seeing each other naked.

His upper body displayed his pure strength, only making me warmer as I stared at him. I pushed a finger into the top of my nightshirt and pulled it forward, blowing down over my chest to try to cool down.

It was hopeless, every part of me was burning up and there was only one way to put out the fire burning within me. I grabbed an ice cube from the freezer. Standing at the corner of the counter half behind Mathieu, I waved to get Luder's attention.

As he glanced up, I showed him the ice cube. I placed it on my neck moving slowly down between my breasts and licking my lips. His eyes lit up as I moved, then I placed my hand down my pants, opened my mouth, and leaned forward. Luder's eyes widened as he shifted on the chair.

Grinning, I joined the men and sat tightly against Luder, holding his leg. He was still shifting, and I felt sure he wanted to go upstairs as much as I wanted to. My fingers tingled as my mind wandered. I wanted to reach up and stroke his chest.

Luder sprung up as Mathieu placed his cup down after taking his last sip. "Thank you for visiting," he said, pulling on my arm so I could stand up. "We will see you tomorrow, it's now time for bed," he added, pushing him towards the door.

I stood holding the door so he could leave. "Goodnight," I added, giving him a push.

"Okay, okay," he mumbled playfully, hitting my hand. "I'll leave, I get the message."

I stood with my hands on my hips until he was out and heading down to the docks. Luder locked the doors and turned to me, beaming.

"I like the steamy, Mrs. Morozov," he said, lifting me into his arms.

Wrapping my arms around his neck and my legs around his waist, I giggled as I replied. "Well then, let's go upstairs and talk about it."

"Is there ice up there as well?" he asked.

"It can be arranged if there isn't," I replied, licking my lips.

There was no need to repeat myself. Luder took the stairs two at a time as he rushed up. Entering the bedroom with speed, he plopped me down on the bed. "Let me have a quick shower, yes?" he asked halfway across the floor on his way to the bathroom.

"Maybe I can join you?" I said in a teasing tone.

Sprinting back, Luder scooped me up and headed to the shower. "Yes, yes, yes," he mumbled as we went.

Placing me down on the vanity, he turned and opened all the taps. It was a large shower with a bench built in at the back and about ten nozzles spraying from all sides. Coming back, he picked me up and swung around, ready to enter the shower.

I burst out laughing as he stopped just in time. "My pants," he mumbled.

"Yes, your pants," I said, breathing deeply as I tried to calm my laughter. "Just lower me so I can do it," I added, taking his face in my hands and kissing him.

Luder lowered my legs so I could stand; his face was filled with a youthful eagerness. Moving my hands slowly down his chest he shivered under my touch. He couldn't stand still as I unbuttoned his pants. He was just as aroused as I was.

It seemed each time we had sex, it only got better and better.

Once the last button was undone, he forcefully pulled his pants down and stepped out of them. His cock was wide awake. It softly bounced as he ushered me into the shower.

161

"Slow down, cowboy," I said as Luder pushed me up against the wall. The water was cooler than I expected, and I shuddered. He turned the taps and warmer water greeted us.

Luder took a deep breath before kissing me. He took my face softly in his hands and kissed me deeply. Moving his hands down my arms and up my sides, I felt my insides turning. Luder grabbed my hips and pulled me closer. Feeling his dick pumping between my legs sent vibrations up my spine.

I lifted one leg and placed it half around him. He welcomed my advance as he firmly held my thigh, kissing me harder. Luder pushed me against the wall before grabbing hold of my butt. Lifting me against the wall, I also wrapped my other leg around his waist.

"Hun," Luder breathed into my neck as his tongue trailed down the side. He lifted me higher and caressed my breasts with his tongue. I arched back in his grip as my senses tingled. He lovingly nibbled at one and then the other, causing a hurricane within me.

I heaved as he continued. I felt my pussy joining his dick as it heated and pumped. "Fuck, me," I whispered, biting his ear lightly.

"Oh, yes," Luder breathed out, lowering me onto his dick. As he filled me with all of him, I dug my nails into his back. My moans filled his neck as I buried my head into it, heaving.

Pushing me to the wall with his chest Luder's hands pulled softly at the edges of my pussy as he pushed deeper into me. I bit down on his neck carefully as I groaned with pleasure. He grabbed my butt and stepped back. Slowly, he sat on the bench against the back wall, placing my feet next to him.

This gave me the freedom to move with him as he raised me up and down on his cock. His hands traveled to my back as I controlled the up and down actions. Tilting back, I allowed him to peck my nipples. Each bite sent new sparks through my body.

Soon, I couldn't move anymore as my body shuddered. Pulling me back to him, Luder took back the reigns. Holding my hips, he lifted and lowered me in quick, hard movements. Lifting my head back, I screamed as I came, feeling him fill me with his warm cum.

Luder heaved as he held me tightly against him. "Hun," he breathed out. "You are amazing."

Standing up after a bit, I smiled lovingly at him. "So are you, baby."

162

I grabbed the sponge and covered him in soap. The sprayers washed it off quicker than I could apply it, and we ended up laughing. After washing, we headed to bed. I felt drained, the day had been very long, but tonight had been excellent.

Laying in his arms walking on his chest with my fingers I spoke, "Luder, can you tell me more about the surprise?"

He smiled and kissed my forehead. "Sleep and soon everything will be here, hun."

I lay still as I felt him falling asleep. Soon, dreamland beckoned me as well.

Epilogue - Luder

Opening my eyes and staring at the ceiling, I stretched out feeling the bed next to me. Skyler was no longer in it. Sitting up quickly, I glanced around the room. She was nowhere to be seen. I listened but didn't hear anyone in the bathroom either. Bunny was also nowhere.

I wondered if the baby woke her so early. Glancing at my watch, I saw it was before six. Getting up, I wondered what she was up to so early. I had hoped to rise before her and make her breakfast again. Now my plans were ruined. She was up before me, and I was sure she was already in the kitchen. That was if she wasn't battling with baby Lucus.

Washing and dressing speedily, I headed to the baby's room first, but it was also empty. Well then, they had to all be downstairs. Yes, I was right, there she was in the kitchen preparing breakfast. She stood at the counter with her back to me, chopping something up. Lucus was seated in his carry chair on the counter chattering away in his own language. He made some gurgling noises as I sneaked up behind Skyler. I enclosed my arms affectionately around her, cupping her breasts.

"Good morning, hun," I breathed over her shoulder, kissing her cheek.

Skyler leaned back against my chest, all sunny. "Good morning, baby," she replied happily. "When are we leaving?" she asked, putting down the knife, and turning in my arms. Bunny came waddling down the stairs, barking, and pushed in between us.

"Morning Bunny, where did you hide?" I said, bending over and ruffling his head.

Standing up, I pulled my eyes together, trying to look serious. "Well, I am waiting for a call first. Therefore, I'm sure we have enough time for breakfast."

Pouting her lips, she leaned forward and kissed me. "Okay, if we must," she added, turning back to the counter.

There was a knock at the glass doors. Glancing up, I saw Mathieu standing there. I moved to unlock the door and allow him in. "Good morning, Mathieu. I take it you found the quarters sufficient?"

"Morning, fine, thanks," Mathieu replied, entering and shaking my hand. He spoke further as he walked to the kitchen counter. "Coffee will be welcome right now."

"You do know all the amenities on the yacht work," I said, shaking my head. He decided to stay on the yacht and with some ground rules, it has been working for us. "There is a kettle and cups. If you need coffee, sugar, or milk, you can just say so."

Skyler smiled and nodded at him as he sat down at the counter. I didn't like the way he appeared to ignore me still, but would speak to him later. I didn't want to upset Skyler, today was a special day. Skyler poured us each a cup as I sat down and continued with breakfast.

"What are the plans for the day?" Mathieu inquired after taking a big gulp of coffee.

"You, dearest Mathieu," I said, patting his back. "You are to report to Ivan's club. There is work still to be done, which you will be assisting with."

"You won't be joining me then?" he asked, lifting an eyebrow.

Sliding off the chair, I walked around the counter and took Skyler around the waist, grinning at him. "We have other things to attend to," I replied.

Skyler beamed at me and gently pulled out of my arms. She fried some eggs and bacon before dishing them up with the salad she had made. She fed the baby while we ate. Once breakfast was done, I called Roman to confirm that the place was ready. He asked if I could give them another couple of hours and suggested I take her for a massage at Irina's parlor.

"Skyler," I said walking back into the kitchen as she was stacking the washer. She stopped and turned, looking at me wide-eyed. "We are going to take a ride first before going to the surprise, dress comfortably."

Putting the last plate down, she pushed the washer door closed and hit start. "Okay," she said strolling past me to head upstairs. She took the baby with her and I could hear her chatting with him as far as she went.

Turning to Mathieu, I spoke. "The driver will take you to the club once you're done." He nodded as he took the last bite and then headed out.

Mathieu was taken to Ivan's club where he would assist in fixing the damage caused by their untimely attack. Most of the damage has been repaired but there was still some work to be done. Ivan had a lot of things he wanted done and Mathieu would be tested during this time.

Turning as the gates closed and Mathieu was on his way, I found Skyler descending the stairs. She was wearing bright pink slacks, a tank top, and a silky jacket. Her golden locks were taken up, with a couple framing her face.

I gasped for air as she took my breath away once again. Her beauty was incomparable, she made my heart skip a beat as she came closer. Maybe we could spend our time in other ways, I considered as she took the last step. I took our baby still in the seat and placed heim down. Drawing Skyler into my arms I kissed her deeply, feeling my blood rush through my veins.

"You are amazing," I breathed out as she pulled back, grinning.

"Yes, thank you, now can we go?" she asked, lifting her eyebrows.

"Or we could stay," I said, grabbing her butt.

"No silly, I want to see the surprise and then, maybe," she added seductively.

Her joy was bubbling over and contagious. I felt like I was floating as I took her hand, picked up the baby in his seat, and walked to the car. Today was going to be special. I hoped to make all her dreams come true.

The drive to Irina's parlor was quicker than I remembered. Stopping at the entrance, we were met with open arms. I assumed Roman had called ahead as Irina, Katrine, and Sam were all waiting for us.

While the women got treated to full body massages, Sergei, Leo, and I had drinks at the bar while babysitting. Sergei visited Ashan before coming there, he said my brother only wanted to get out. Knowing Ashan, I could imagine how he was performing. He has never been one for staying still or doing nothing, especially for three months.

166

Even though he was a couple of years younger, he has been more willful than I ever was. By the time the ladies were done, we had about three drinks.

Skyler flung her arms around my neck and kissed me long and hard. "That was so exhilarating," she said. "I feel so much better. We have decided to do this every week if that will be okay?"

Smiling, I nodded at her. It was time to call Roman. I confirmed that the premises were ready.

"Right," I spoke as we all walked to the door. "It's time to go; we'll see you later?" I added, shaking Sergei's and Leo's hands.

After agreeing to a get-together at Sergei and Irina's place, we left later. Skyler was shifting in her seat as I drove slowly along. Her anticipation must be killing her, but I was enjoying tormenting her a little.

"Can't we go faster," she asked as I stopped longer than needed at a stop sign.

Grinning at her, I replied, dragging out my words. "I suppose we could try."

"Luder," she said in a pitched voice.

"Okay, okay, I'll go a little faster, but there is a child in the car," I replied as she was about to pounce me out of excitement.

I had been going up and down the streets delaying the trip. Turning down towards the beach, Skyler looked at me pushing her lips out and bringing her eyes together.

"Are we going home, is it at home?" she inquired.

Laughing, I replied softly. "No, it's not, but it is close by."

Skyler's mouth fell open as she pushed her jaw down. "Really, and we've been driving up and down all this time."

"I was exploring the area," I replied.

About two blocks from the house, I pulled up to large Iron gates and pressed the horn. The gates opened slowly, and I pulled in, before us lay the massive building with its two glass sliding doors.

"What's this? Where are we?" Skyler questioned as I got out and moved to open her door.

Holding out my hand, she took it and got out. Standing side by side, I grinned at her. "Skyler," I started turning her to face me. "This building symbolizes the start of something truly great."

She glanced at the building and then back at me. "Okay, so what is it?"

I turned her to face the building stepping in behind her. Leaning forward as I wrapped my arms around her, I whispered. "This is yours, for your own animal rescue center. Or whatever you want to do with it."

Skyler looked at me, her lovely eyes wide. "Mine?" she uttered. I could hear her voice disappearing as reality set in. "Mine?" she shouted, running towards the doors. She was bouncing up and down before the doors as she turned, beaming at me.

Grabbing our son from the car, I walked over. I nodded in agreement before handing her the keys. Skyler fumbled at the lock and pushed the doors open. She ran into the vast openness of the entrance and reception area.

I had decided to leave this room empty so she could do the décor to her licking. "Skyler," I said, walking to her where she was turning in circles, screaming excitedly.

Stopping her turns and taking her into my arms I whispered into her ear. "We're not alone."

"What," she protested, pushing me back and looking around.

To each side of the reception area were three doors. To the back was another set of double glass doors leading out to the backyard. Skyler walked forward towards the glass doors when the side doors all opened.

"Surprise," the family shouted together as they stepped into the room.

Skyler's hands flew up to her mouth as she looked from one to the other. Her face turned crimson as her earlier action dawned on her. On one side, we had Roman, Sergei, and Leo with their better halves. On the other side were Ivan, Nikolai, and Aleksei with their wives.

From the back, Yuri came in with Oleg, the father of the family. It was the first time she met so many at once. Skyler grabbed hold of my arm as I turned to introduce her to everyone. I began with Oleg, who was thrilled to finally meet her.

Skyler suddenly appeared shy as she hung on my arm while we made a round through the room. Once all the introductions were done, the family gathered outside at the back where they had set up a big lunch for everyone.

Roman and Karine led Skyler and me through the other rooms while Sam looked after the children. There were three consultation rooms, an observation room, and a kennel room. The kennel room was fitted with large areas closed in to keep sick animals overnight. Plus, there was a kitchen.

In each consultation room was a table, a soft and hard table to be used for examinations, and some storage cabinets. The storage in each room included one normal and one cold to keep the medicines in.

Skyler gasped as we entered each room and had to touch everything. Her disbelief was prominent and stirred my feelings. I just wanted to take her in my arms and hold her tight. She was like a child who had just received the greatest gift ever.

Once we had been through the entire place, it was time to join the family for lunch. Walking out with her on my arm, beaming at the world. I felt a burning within. I wanted to be alone with her but knew we had to endure them for a while longer. After all, everyone assisted in making this project a reality.

After a round of visiting each table, snacking here and there, Skyler seemed to ease up. She joined the women under a big tree where the little ones were playing. This allowed me to convey my gratitude to everyone for their part.

We shared a couple of drinks and talked about all that had happened throughout the year so far. It was nice catching up with everyone and sharing with Oleg. Soon, the sun started to set, and one by one, the family said their goodbyes and left. After cleaning up, Roman, Karine, Sergei, and Irina also left. Karine and Roman took our Lucus with them as we wanted some alone time.

Skyler and I locked the back door and went from room to room, turning off the unneeded lights. Entering the small kitchen, I switched on the radio that Roman had insisted we install. Skyler looked at me in awe as I pulled her close.

"This was a lovely day, don't you think?" I said, twirling her across the reception area.

Skyler lifted her face to the ceiling as she laughed. The vision of her tickled all my senses, slowly waking the beast. We were eventually alone. My heart skipped a beat as I drew her back into my arms.

"You are so amazing," I breathed out, staring into her soul.

Skyler came forward quickly. As our lips met, I felt sparks igniting the fires I held inside.

Coming up for breath, she spoke softly, gasping for air. "Want to christen the place with me?"

"Oh, most definitely," I replied, picking her up into my arms and walking to the nearest consulting room.

Entering the room, I stopped for a second scanning the options before deciding the softer table would be more suitable. Laying her down on the table, I decided to try something new.

Rambling through the closet, I found soft bandages. Holding them up, I glanced at Skyler. "Want to be tied up?" I asked softly.

Giggling, she replied in a joyous tone. "Sure, why not."

I walked over and tied both her hands to the table's sides. I ensured that they weren't too tight but would suffice in holding her hands in place. "Now then," I said, standing back. "Let's get rid of your clothes first."

I should have done this before tying her, I thought to myself as I pulled her pants down and dropped them to the floor. The table was longer than she was. Pushing her feet up and bending her knees, I could comfortably rest them on the table.

Skyler chuckled as I moved. Unzipping her jacket, I was faced with removing the crop top. Grabbing the scissors from the physician's table, I made a smooth cut through the crop top. Pulling the two pieces sideways, exposing her perfectly shaped breasts stirred my desire more.

"You having fun yet?" I whispered as I kissed her breasts.

Skyler nodded her head, "Yes, very much baby."

With her practically naked displayed on the table, I grabbed the stethoscope and stripped the paper off. "Mmm…," I said, turning to her. "Now, if I remember correctly, these two pieces go in my ears," I said, stepping closer. "And this part goes here," I added placing the end on her clitoris.

Skyler gasped as the cold stethoscope touched her. "No silly," she replied, tittering. "It goes between my breasts."

Looking at her grinning, I tapped the end carefully on the back. "You sure," I said as she breathed in deeply. "Maybe," I added, sliding it further down. "Maybe, it goes in here," I said, slipping it into her vagina.

Skyler breathed in deeply and pushed her bottom up into the air as the stethoscope entered her. "Oh, baby," she breathed out slowly.

"You still good?" I asked, moving to her side and pecking at her breast.

"Yes," she said looking at me. "The things you do to me drive me wild."

Pulling the surgical tray closer, I pick up the surgical clamps. Holding them out above her, I spoke softly. "You want to try these?"

Skyler turned her head from side to side, examining them before nodding and giggling. I gradually clamped one onto each nipple.

"Do they hurt?" I inquired, studying her face.

Skyler shook her head from side to side, biting her lower lips. "No, they are giving me a tingling sensation through." Pushing the trolley aside, I delicately pulled at them, watching her reaction. Skyler closed her eyes, moaning as she slightly shifted left and right.

Moving back down and standing between her legs, I felt my dick fighting the limitations of my pants. It was time for me to get rid of my clothing as well, I thought, stepping out of them and pulling my shirt over my head.

Placing my hands on her hips, I slowly push them up to her breasts as I lean in, licking her pussy. Skyler shifted around my head, groaning as I sought out her clitoris. Once I sucked it into my mouth, I lightly pulled at the clamps.

Skyler lifted her pussy into my face as her moans became louder. I waited for her to relax and lower herself back down before continuing. This time, I nibbled her clitoris twisting the clams from side to side. Skyler panted as she lifted up and I felt her spraying over my chin.

"Oh, baby," she breathed out as I let go. "Baby, fuck me, fuck me now."

My dick was pounding between my legs and more than ready to consume her. Pulling her down towards me I stepped closer to the edge of the table. It was a perfect height. As her feet came off the edge and her butt lay on the edge, I penetrated her.

Skyler let out a scream of pleasure as I swiftly moved in and out of her, feeling my own pleasure rising with every move. She moaned, bit her lips, and screamed over and over as I pushed harder and deeper.

I filled her with all of me as my legs began to shake, and my body trembled from pleasure. Lowering my head to her chest, my breathing came out jagged, I released the clamps and untied her hands. We were sweating in equal amounts as she placed her hands on my head, trying to catch her breath.

"Baby," she breathed out after a while. "I love you."

Lifting myself from her, I kissed her stomach and held out my hands to help her upright. We would have to get home to shower as the building only had toilets and basins. Once we were dressed, we locked up and headed home.

"Tomorrow, I'll have the bedding washed that is on that table," Skyler said, beaming at me.

"Yes," I replied, pulling into our driveway.

Mathieu was sitting on the steps waiting. "Oh no," Skyler said, blushing. "I forgot he was here."

We chuckled, glancing at each other. "It's okay," I added. "You go on up, I'll sort it out."

Skyler greeted Mathieu in the passing and headed inside. "Evening," Mathieu said as I stood before him.

"Evening, if there is anything you need, ask Ivan and he will provide it for you," I replied passing him and stopping at the door. Glancing back, I pushed my hand through my hair. "You should also ask him about living arrangements. Good night."

Mathieu stood there astounded as I closed the door and headed upstairs. Skyler had already drawn the bath and was waiting for me to wash her back.

We were both tired as we got into bed. I noticed she fell asleep with a wide smile on her face. I was glad that I could make her happy and planned to do so forever.

Over the next couple of weeks, Skyler and I managed to add the finishing touches to the shelter. We also hired veterinarians, nurses, and other staff. It wasn't even a month later, and the shelter opened its doors. Skyler named it The Luder Sky.

Ashan returned and assisted us where he could. His shoulder and arm healed very well, according to the doctor. But for extra safety, he decided to get two dogs as well. He trained them to attack on order, and strangely enough, he even allowed them to sleep inside.

Over the next couple of months, we settled into a place of our own next to the shelter.

Mathieu settled in nicely with Ivan's men. He eventually moved to a place of his own, closer to the club and further from us. Which was good for us all.

Skyler, with the help of Karine, Irina, and Sam, decorated the room next to ours for baby Lucus and even added a door between the two rooms.

Karine, Sam, and Skyler started spending more and more time together. I was glad that the family accepted her so openly.

By the time our boy was old enough, we were ready. Everyone came over to meet little Lucus on the 100th day and took turns holding him. Oleg blessed him with a silver cross and welcomed his life to our family. We gathered in the yard for a full celebration of life.

THE END

ABOUT LEXI ASHER

Lexi Asher gave up a promising career in the medical field to focus entirely on her family—and her writing. She lives in the beautiful, luscious Virginia countryside with her husband, 3 young children and 4 pets.

The Ashers' rustic cottage is bustling with activity all day long, so when Lexi wants to get her head down and let her creative juices flow, she will often take refuge in their beautifully ornate conservatory where Lexi does most of her writing.

When it comes to love, Lexi is a big believer in second chances—sometimes you just meet the right person at the wrong time. So, her stories often feature old flames that are reignited and broken hearts that are mended. But is love really better the second time around? Well, read and find out!

BOOKS BY LEXI ASHER

"Morozov Bratva" Series

The Russian Bratva of Miami has three rules: solve problems with violence, paint the streets with blood, and break hearts at will. They're not nice, they're not gentle, and they don't compromise. But behind closed doors, they'll show you what ruthless love really means.

Kidnapped by the Bratva

A Secret Baby by the Bratva

Pregnant by the Bratva

Sold to the Bratva

Forbidden by the Bratva

Surrogate for the Bratva

Bullied by the Bratva

Betrayed by the Bratva

Auctioned to the Bratva

Hostage of the Bratva

"Small Town Billionaires" Series

Pretend for the Billionaire

The Billionaire's Baby

The Billionaire's Next Door Neighbor

"The Crenshaw Billionaire Brothers" Series

Billionaire Brothers is where grumpiness and pain give way to romance and love. These loaded heirs may seem to have it all: money to burn, looks to die for, women to spoil. But it takes a special someone, a magical spark to reveal the real man behind the facade.

Grumpy Billionaire

Bossy Billionaire

Daddy Billionaire

"Lakeside Love" Series

Riverroad is a small town where everyone knows everyone, where the guy you've known since childhood turns into the hottest hunk around, where friends become lovers, and where everyday interactions between neighbors might just turn into steamy encounters when you least expect it...

Chasing A Second Chance

Chasing The Doctor Next Door

Chasing A Fake Wedding

Chasing The Cowboy

Printed in Dunstable, United Kingdom